IN THE NAME OF THE FATHER

IN THE NAME OF THE FATHER

Stories about Priests

Collected by
Michael F. McCauley

THE THOMAS MORE PRESS
Chicago, Illinois

ISBN 0-88347-147-7

ACKNOWLEDGMENTS

Grateful acknowledgment is made for permission to reprint the following copyrighted material:

Richard Sullivan, "Saturday Nocturne"
Reprinted by permission of *The Yale Review*, December 1945. Copyright © 1945 by Yale University Press.

Mark Helprin, "Leaving the Church"
Reprinted by permission of Alfred A. Knopf, Inc. From *A Dove of the East and Other Stories* by Mark Helprin. Copyright

CONTENTS

PREFACE

THERE is a perennial curiosity about life behind the rectory door. Priests are, after all, different from the rest of us. They are, most notably, celibate. And this difference, incomprehensible to many, enhances the aura of otherworldliness that has attached to priests—and survives to this day despite the more down-to-earth priests of the postconciliar church. Deep down, however, whether they are associates or pastors or monsignors or bishops or cardinals, priests have the same foibles, failings, and shortcomings that we all have.

From time to time, it is reassuring to us to be reminded that Father is equally battered and buffeted as he works out his own salvation. Some of the world's most superbly talented authors have truly appreciated that those who are most visibly dedicated to religion are also most humanly living in this often banal world. The poignant authenticity of their descriptions will almost convince readers that the stories collected here must have been written from within the rectory. Yet, without exception, these stories have been written from outside the rectory. Thematic to all of them is the simple yet profound truth that priests have no guarantee of superhuman powers; it is not necessarily easier to be a good Christian just because one says yes to ordination.

Ordination, of course, has been pursued for a variety of reasons—some noble, some not so noble; some selfless, some not so selfless. Many priests, to be sure, have been motivated by the desire to save their own souls and the souls of others through the administration of the sacraments. In Morley Callaghan's "A Sick Call," an ailing Catholic woman's husband—who was "very bigoted and hated all church people"—will not let the priest administer the last sacrament. The priest resorts to a slight deception in order to hear the sick woman's confession. Although the priest rejoiced "amiably to think he had so successfully ministered to one who had strayed from the faith and had called out to him at the last moment," he could not help wondering whether he had come between husband and wife. "What a beauty there was to his staunch love for her," he thought. "But it was just a pagan beauty, of course." As the priest ponders the nature of this beauty, "for some reason he felt inexpressibly sad."

Temptations of the flesh are not restricted to laypersons, as countless confessors and moral theologians have realized for ages. Mark Helprin writes of an old pastor from Arizona, in Rome for the Second Vatican Council, who is confronted by demons and doubts he thought had long ago left him. A failed love affair with a young Radcliffe student floods his memory. He had been a young priest studying in Rome when the two of them had run away to Switzerland. The affair had not lasted long but it had nearly destroyed him when she left. He survived, however, and after forty years of exile in the desert of Arizona, ends up in a Rome hospital where he finally finds peace and great courage—and salvation.

Although a host of theological issues are, like celibacy and priestly commitment, far weightier than generation gap, Richard Sullivan's "Saturday Nocturne" penetrates beyond the mere tension between a pastor and his assistant. The young priest, fresh from ordination, is outraged by both racial violence in the town and pastoral inactivity in the face of injustice. The injustice is by no means eliminated by these two priests, but they come to a sense of mutual respect, understanding, and companionship as they work together on attacking racial prejudice.

J. F. Powers, in the slyly satirical, quietly humorous "The Presence of Grace," perceptively portrays the curious, creative tensions between a greying dormouse of a pastor and his recently ordained zealous curate. Young Father Fabre finds the old pastor dotty and bewildering, at best. But when the young curate is reported by the indignant ladies of the Altar and Rosary

Society to have entered into a compromising situation, it is the taciturn old pastor who triumphs. His coup is brought about not by pulling rank or delivering an edifying homily, but by uttering a few well-chosen monosyllabic words. Once again, a special grace, which somehow supercedes individual eccentricities and failings, bridges a gap.

A gap of a different sort exists in William Trevor's "Death in Jerusalem." The gap is between two Irish-born brothers—one a priest in San Francisco, the other a bachelor in County Tipperary who runs the family business and takes care of his aged mother. Both men are duty-bound, yet they interpret their respective duties in vastly different ways, ways that lead one to replace his lifelong admiration for the other with hatred. Trevor probes for the true meaning of duty, commitment, responsibility, and familial loyalty in the characters of these two brothers on pilgrimage to the Holy Land—a land of ironic mockery and disappointment and self-reproach.

Disappointment and self-reproach are not to be found in Frank O'Connor's classic portrayal of the 86-year-old Bishop of Moyle, the Most Reverend Dr. Gallogly. "Vanity" celebrates, in the person of the bishop, the things that O'Connor himself most admired—fortitude, wit, courage, and human cussedness. As might be expected, the bishop's own silly vanity—"the great temptation of religious people"—more than once is his undoing.

Similar to O'Connor's vain bishop is the monsignor in Charles Healy's "A Question of Degree." Msgr. Carey was a practical man, an administrator, the pastor of a choice parish. One Saturday afternoon he quickly and matter-of-factly accepts the fact of his own stigmata. Since no one is worthy to experience the stigmata, Msgr. Carey, practical man that he was, reasoned that the whole matter was a question of the degree of unworthiness—whether he was less unworthy than anyone else. Struggling with this miracle, the monsignor bumbles amiably as he attempts to become the model stigmatist. Along the way, he perceives the role of providence in his own destiny and realizes that although he is the boss in his parish, he's not *the* boss.

The eight well-crafted short stories collected here give revealing glimpses not just behind the rectory door, but into the hearts and souls of the priests who live there. Many recall a time in the church before parish priests had to be professionals, before priests had any formal training in clinical-pastoral skills or counseling or group dynamics or business administration. Zeal, sincerity, and "a good heart"—not professionalism—characterize these priests. They are, on the whole, competent and sympathetic, nonetheless. More important, these priests are human beings whose spiritual experiences, fascinating confusions, essential loneliness—even crises—resonate within our lives because they are no more and no less than men of God.

Michael F. McCauley

SATURDAY NOCTURNE
by Richard Sullivan

AFTER the angelus rang that Saturday evening, Father Shay heard the confessions of the two people still in line. He waited a few minutes then, as he always did, in case there were others coming; he always had the feeling that there might be just one more, and it would have worried him to leave that one unheard. But tonight when no one else came he left the confessional willingly. He had been in it since three-thirty that afternoon, and his homely young face was red and damp over his wilted collar. Outside, hurrying across the yard from church to rectory, he pulled the hot cassock away from his chest and took deep breaths of the cool twilight air. He was a large young man with a wide mouth and a twisted, flattened nose; he moved with long steps and swinging shoulders.

When he came in the back door, Mrs. Bell, the housekeeper, was in the kitchen, and he heard Father Lordy in the dining room.

"Has he started eating?"

"Well," said Mrs. Bell; she looked at the alarm clock on the window sill, "it's a quarter after six."

"Tell him I'll be there as soon as I wash."

When he got to the table, Father Lordy was at

his pie and coffee, and was reading the evening paper. Shuler's Bake Shop, Father Shay thought, peering at the pie; why doesn't she ever bake it herself? He said grace and sat down. Mrs. Bell had put the platter of cold cuts and the other dishes over close to his place, and he started helping himself.

"Lots of excitement in town this afternoon," Father Lordy said, without looking up from his paper.

"Oh?"

"Riot out at the ball park." Head down, he glanced up between white eyebrows and silver-rimmed glasses; his voice was gruff; hesitating, he seemed to speculate on how the young priest would take serious news. "Negroes," he said.

"What started it?" cried Father Shay sharply. His fork made a brittle clatter on his plate; he stared across the table.

"Ah, it's one of those things," said Father Lordy. "You can't tell *how* it started." He sat back and shoved the newspaper out on the table. Father Shay hastily reached for it. "No, no, it's not in the paper. I heard it on the radio just now. Somebody pushed somebody else when they were all standing up for the seventh-inning stretch—"

"The lucky seventh!" cried Father Shay.

"And four people were hurt—"

"All Negroes?" Father Shay's face was dark and accusing.

"Three, I think."

"Yes, you see! Three out of four!"

"There was nobody seriously hurt," said Father Lordy. "They got it under control so fast I don't suppose you could really call it a riot."

"But the same thing's happening all over the country!" cried Father Shay. "It's not just that nobody was hurt—it's the *idea* of the thing!"

"Anyhow, it wasn't like some of those big riots in the cities. It was all over in twenty minutes."

"But these things *grow*!" Father Shay was terribly upset, as if he had been offended personally.

"It's a nasty thing," said Father Lordy, shaking his head. "It's the first time anything like that has happened in this town in all the time I've been here." He stood up and made the sign of the cross. Then for a moment he hesitated as if he had something more to say about the trouble at the ball park; but when Father Shay looked at him expectantly he only frowned and shook his head again.

"It's enough to make a man sick!" burst out Father Shay. "It's shameful! Why, there are people who think Negroes have no souls! No wonder there are riots!"

"I know, I know," said Father Lordy. "I'll be in on the couch," he said. "Call me when you go over."

Father Shay ate his supper broodingly. He had been ordained just two months, and this was his first parish. In the few weeks he had been here, he had frequently felt inexperienced, so that he had been ashamed of his own youth and foolishness; but now his sense of inexperience made him resentful. He didn't know anything about Negroes, he was ready to admit it; he didn't even know any Negroes. But he did know injustice when he saw it, and in this town he had seen it from the first. It was not a very large town, and there were not a great many Negroes here, proportionately, but those who were here, he thought, were being pushed around: they were paying exorbitant rents for foul housing; some of the factories refused them work entirely; others took them on but carefully kept them down; and there was a feeling in the air, a vague, unphrased but strong feeling, that this was the way things were supposed to be; at least no one said that this was *not* the right way to have things.

He had been shocked by the news Father Lordy had given him. But now, brooding, he felt more deeply shocked by what seemed to him the casualness, the indifference of the old priest. Oh, it was probably true that the extraordinary surge of people to town to work in the factories had made disturbances like this at the ball park more likely; they were effects of the times. Yet underneath them, there was a kind of permanent and horrible evil. Father Lordy seemed to have no sense of it, no sense of what was happening. He'd been pastor here for nineteen years now; he was probably so used to the town that he couldn't see it freshly any more. But he ought to see it freshly; that was his obligation. The acceptance of injustice seemed to Father Shay almost worse than injustice itself. Bolting his supper, he felt a passion of bitterness and urgency. "No pie, Mrs. Bell," he told her when she started to clear away dishes.

"Coffee, Father?" Mrs. Bell slanted her eyebrows in hurt indifference about the pie.

"What time is it?" He started fumbling for his watch.

"You have twenty minutes."

"All right. Coffee."

When he went in to call Father Lordy five minutes later, he was still bitter and urgent. "That rioting at the ball park," he said. "You know we ought to do something about it!"

Father Lordy sat up on the old leather couch; he was in his shirt sleeves; he combed his white hair with his fingers and fastened his collar, then reached for his cassock. "It's a nasty thing," he said.

"I'd like to preach about it tomorrow."

"What would you say?"

"Well,...it's unchristian...it's beastly!"

"Look, young Father Gene," said the old

priest, buttoning his cassock buttons with big deliberate fingers. "I know how you feel. I've been thinking, too. But it's not enough just to say it's bad. That's fine, to say it, of course...but what are you going to do about it?" He paused and sniffed, almost in embarrassment. "You see, I know as well as you do that it's unchristian. It's evil, that's what it is, evil, and there are generations of evil behind it. That makes it hard"...he shook his head..."generations of evil. I'm troubled by it, I admit. It bursts out this way all of a sudden." He paused. "I don't know just what to do about it," he said.

The two of them had walked together through the kitchen, past Mrs. Bell clattering at the sink; now they were going across the backyard in the dusk to the church. The clock in the steeple started striking seven as they walked. Father Shay was silent. He doesn't know what to do, he thought, so he won't do anything: the slow, passive defeat. He felt himself drifting into a deep black melancholy. But he was going to do something. Maybe he didn't know just what to do either, but he was going to do something.

At the side door of the church Father Lordy cleared his throat gruffly. "Maybe it's just that I'm an old man," he said. "I won't say you shouldn't mention it tomorrow. Only be careful. It's too important to be careless and emotional about. Think it over and we'll talk about it later tonight. I'd like to talk about it with you." He opened the door. "If I knew what to say I might mention it tomorrow myself," he said gloomily.

Father Shay bounded up the stone steps with the sudden conviction that he had won the old man over, that he had made a conversion. He shook his big clenched fists tightly at his sides. If Father Lordy had been another kind of man, he would have thumped him on the shoulder at that moment. As it was he grinned happily, his white teeth bright in the dusk against his rough red face. "Thank you, Father," he said.

Hurrying up the south aisle to his confessional, he heard the old priest's heavy footsteps clumping on the rubber matting of the north aisle, like echoes of his own; there was a kind of companionship, a kind of sympathy, in the mingling sounds. As he stooped to get into his confessional Father Shay felt exhilarated and eager. Tomorrow, he thought. He tried to recall just what he'd said to Father Lordy, but it didn't really matter; it was probably the way you said a thing as much as the thing itself, anyhow. If people could be made to *see* that a thing was wrong, if it was made *clear* to them, they would change; they *had* to change. At the seminary a priest had once told Father Shay that he had a too great confidence in the perfectibility of human nature. He did have; he knew it now, sitting in the confessional; he felt a quick exuberance; he was glad of his own great confidence. Tomorrow he'd make them *see*. But now people coming to confession got in the way of his plans. He had to concentrate on them; he took all his obligations very seriously.

In a little while he thought of combining penances with his own intentions. "For your holy penance say three Hail Mary's for the spread of Christian charity among all men," he whispered to one person through the white screened grill. To the next, "For your holy penance say five Our Father's and five Hail Mary's for the spread of justice and charity in our town. Now make a good act of contrition." To one woman he gave a decade of the rosary to be said for all oppressed people; to what sounded like a young man, the litany of the saints for grace to love and respect his fellow men. It gave him a deep satisfaction to tie these penances in with his own urgent concern. It seemed to him an effectual thing to get prayers said; he wondered if perhaps it was not more effectual than his preaching tomorrow would be. Reflecting on that, he decided that what he was really doing was making a fine practical combination of prayer and good works.

An old man whose false teeth smacked and clopped was in the box, but Father Shay's attention wandered a little. He thought of the rioting at the ball park that day, and imagined himself there, in the shouting and fury, quelling the mob. With his head bent sideways towards the grill he listened to the old man's mumbling, but at the same time he was surrounded by rioting Negroes who did not understand that he was not their enemy; they were cursing and shrieking, a ring of dark men and women; they were grabbing at his outstretched arms, expecting him to fight back, but he would not; they beat at him; his breath in the confessional quickened. He listened to the old man, but at the same time he was making a heroic sacrifice of himself. "It's all right!" he was crying in his imagination to the mob. "Go ahead! You're right, you're right! You've stood enough—take it out on me! I'm white—take it out on me!"

Beyond the screen, the false teeth smacked once finally, and the voice was silent. Father Shay shook his head sharply. Remotely, with a sudden drop of emotion, he pulled himself from the heroic vision and concentrated on what the old man had said. He murmured for a moment; then, "For your holy penance say three Our Father's for the sake of the oppressed people of our town." He heard the grunting and scraping, then the soft, woody thump of the confessional door—usually it didn't slam, the one going out holding it open for the one coming in. He waited; no one came; in the darkness his watch glowed green: 8:40. He stuck his head out of his own little door and saw that the church was empty, and Father Lordy was gone, his confessional door wide open.

Presumption, he thought, returning to his dream of the rioting. It had been so real, so exciting, that now in memory it was like an actual experience. But a person would really have no right to offer himself to a mob that way. All the same they deserved a victim. But it would really be inciting them to sin, to offer yourself to a mob. A doubt hung in his mind, though; he went into the vestibule to switch off lights. It wouldn't have to be sinful; it would depend on the way you did it; he wondered how martyrs felt ahead of their martyrdom. If you did something like that in complete honesty, out of justice...but then they'd probably not attack you at all; they'd understand and be changed. He saw himself in the centre of a dark converted throng, the voices dying, the fists unclenched, the once angry faces awe-struck; and standing in the vestible he swallowed once, hard.

The front door rattled open; he turned; it was the janitor come to lock up.

"All through, Father?"

"Looks like it, Joe."

The janitor slid a bolt on the door. "See the Sox took the second one in the double-header," he said.

"They *did?*" Father Shay suddenly remembered that he had forgotten to tune in on the baseball scores at supper time. "What was...?"

"Eight to two," Joe said.

"Ah they start at the end of the season," said Father Shay. "They never get going until the end!"

He went out one of the side doors, lighted a cigarette, and started across the school yard towards the rectory. Gravel crunched beneath his shoes; the sky overhead was massed with moonlit clouds, a bright exciting sky. Again he saw the imaginary mob about him, and again he offered himself to it. "You've stood enough! Take it out on me!" As he walked across the crunching gravel he stretched his arms out and threw his head back, whispering the words.

He couldn't find Father Lordy in the house. He finally went down the back hall and tapped on Mrs. Bell's door. She opened it so quickly that she surprised him.

"Well, he made some phone calls, Father, and then he went out at eight o'clock. He told me to be sure and tell you he'd be back a little after nine."

"Oh," said Father Shay. "All right, Mrs. Bell."

He went up the back stairs to his own room. For a moment he stood in front of the dresser, frowning absently at the still unframed photograph of his class at the seminary. Then he slowly took off his cassock and collar, opened the bottom dresser drawer and took out an old blue sweater. He pulled it over his head; then, smoothing his hair with his hands, he glanced at himself in the mirror. In the heavy crew-necked sweater, with the fuzzy twisting ends of yarn at the shoulder where he had ripped it that time two years ago playing touch football, he looked curiously tough and burly. He peered at his big raw face, his twisted nose. Enough to scare a dog, he thought. He turned and went out, down the back stairs.

"Mrs. Bell," he called, "will you please tell Father Lordy I'll be back in twenty minutes?"

She opened the door again before he was ready for her. He saw the way she looked at the sweater. "That is, if he gets back before I do," he said.

"I'll tell him," she said, and her eyebrows slanted ever so slightly as she closed the door.

In the front hall he switched off the light, then waited at the door for a moment to see if anybody was going by outside. When he had first come here, a few weeks ago, he had put on this old sweater one afternoon, intending to run a couple of miles as a workout; but Father Lordy had stopped him at this very door. "You're not going outside in the broad daylight in that rig," he told him. "Have you no dignity?" Father

Shay had explained meekly that he honestly needed the exercise; without it he put on weight quickly and got sluggish; he had always led a strenuous life. It was arranged then that he take his workouts at night, when no one was likely to see him in his disreputable sweater. "There are ways to do a thing," Father Lordy said, "and there are ways *not* to do a thing." He had been standing right here in this hall when he had said it, and it had been impossible to tell what he was thinking. Going out the doorway now, Father Shay wondered whether the old priest considered these nightly workouts ridiculous or whether he really approved of them. It was a little hard to be sure of Father Lordy. He jogged down the sidewalk wondering.

He had by now established a regular course for his nightly run: six blocks down to a little park, a block square; three times around this block and the six blocks home made two miles, as he figured. But the park was so small that he wondered sometimes if his figuring wasn't a little generous.

Tonight he went the first few blocks slowly, loosening up. He held his head down when he passed street lights or people, because, of course, he agreed with what Father Lordy had said about dignity. Still, he wasn't going to stop running just because people might find it amusing and talk. He had always had a dread of being afraid, of being shamed into a kind of dishonorable prudence.

He was running at a good moderate clip when he came to the park. A couple of little boys whom he recognized as belonging to the parish were playing around a water bubbler at the corner. As he ran at them out of the darkness they dodged into the street, startled. He kept his face turned away, and tried to imagine how he looked to them. Behind him he heard them run across the street out of the park.

He slowed down a little, staring at the black trees and the spottily moonlit grass. Often when he came here at night, there were people scattered about on the benches in the park, but now the place seemed deserted. He wondered suddenly if the trouble at the ball park could be responsible, people not wanting to come out tonight after a thing like that. But the idea seemed farfetched. His feet made quick regular patting noises on the cement sidewalk, and as he began the second round his breath was coming deep and easy and he pushed his stride.

Then ahead of him, in the dark tunnelled stretch at one edge of the park, where small thorn trees grew for about twenty feet close on each side of the walk, he saw a man standing. It startled him, to see this unexpected figure dark in the darkness, moonlight behind him—he hadn't been there before, unless he'd been hiding, and it was such a very small park that he couldn't have come in without being seen. Father Shay kept running, and the man suddenly laughed, a clear but intimate laugh, as if someone had just told a joke; at the same instant a girl stood up from a bench were she had been sitting—a bench in a kind of nook among the thorn trees; Father Shay hadn't seen it before—and she laughed too, rather raucously, with the man.

The priest was now about ten paces from them; he swerved onto the narrow strip of grass, giving them the sidewalk. He felt at once that they were laughing at him. They had been watching him here, they had recognized him, and now they were laughing. Resentful, angry, embarrassed, he kept his head down and ran; there were roots twisting up out of the grass; he tripped on one, and grunting furiously plunged forward almost at the feet of the two on the sidewalk.

"O-oh-h!" the girl cried. "Sa-a-ay!" said the man. For an instant they both stood back, almost as if they were afraid of him. Then—"Help him up, Sonny! See if he's hurt!" the girl said. The man hesitated an instant, then stooped.

Looking up, still angrier, breathing hard, Father Shay saw first the man's white shirt looming above him, then the dark apprehensive face, then the girl's face: they were Negroes. With a kind of dazed clarity he understood at once their air of caution, their hesitancy; they were worried by what had happened this afternoon; he saw how he must have looked to them a moment before, big, unknown, lumbering up out of the darkness; he even knew how threatening his face must look right now, and he struggled to smile, to seem friendly. Getting up, the man's hand under his arm, he remembered his proud dream of the riot, himself against the mob; and he was humiliated by the irony of this moment. These people were not attacking him; they were helping him. He felt foolish and ashamed. Lurching onto his feet, he clutched the man's arm gratefully. Close up he saw the girl's face, staring, saw her eyebrows shoot up and her mouth open. "Sonny!" she cried to the man. "Watch out!" Father Shay knew then what was coming; he wanted to stop it; with a fierce, desperate gesture he thrust out his hand towards the girl. "No, no!" he cried. But the man had already broken from his grasp, the girl was already running; the man darted after her. "Wait!" shouted Father Shay. "Wait!" Frantic, he started after them. "Please, wait!"

But they were yards ahead, running wildly, the man looking back. Father Shay stopped, stood there on the sidewalk; his homely face twisted grotesquely, and he beat one fist into the palm of the other hand. "O God," he said, "O dear

God!" Things reeled through his mind: the hopeless enormity of their feeling, and its unexpectedness, the generations, the generations, too important to be careless about, and Father Lordy shaking his head, saying, "Only I don't know what to do," and the incredible enormity of injustice, the impossible strength of evil.

He watched the Negroes to the far corner of the park; when they crossed the street he turned and started walking towards home. His mind worked in dull slow whirls, over and over. With awful clarity he realized that he was a fool. Going to straighten things out, zip, like that, with a neat little sermon in the morning. A serene fool, full of good will, of course, and full of pride and of easy heroics of the imagination. In the darkness his lips drew tight and trembled like a boy's under strong shame. He was walking too slowly—he made himself take brisker steps. He felt his mind thump heavily over, and a question which had been murky and unphrased now came into focus: What was he going to say to Father Lordy when he got back? "I'd like to talk it over with you," Father Lordy had said. After all, he thought, feeling himself wince—after all, preaching in this parish isn't much use anyway. He knew that he was excusing himself, but he was so flattened and empty that he didn't care, for just that moment. Still, he thought wearily, something still has to be done. This hadn't changed the necessity; it was more urgent than ever now, really, to do something—and harder than ever. Thinking of the difficulty, he felt powerless, as in a nightmare.

When he came very quietly in the front door he saw Father Lordy on the old leather couch in the front room. He was sitting up straight, in street clothes, reading his breviary. Father Shay tiptoed down the dark hall.

"That you, Father?" The old priest's voice was sharp and impatient.

Father Shay turned and came back. When he looked into the room he said nothing.

"Come in! Come in! I've been waiting for you!" Father Lordy didn't seem to notice the sweater; he pointed with his breviary at a chair. "Sit down, I'll be through with this in a minute."

Father Shay sat down. He watched the light glint dully on the crinkled toes of his shoes, side by side on the thin brown carpet; then he looked up at the old priest's face. Frowning intently, Father Lordy was whispering the words of his office; his lips made little loose quick movements, and his eyelids fluttered behind his glasses. He was sitting up very straight, the book in both hands before him; he seemed eager to be finished, as if he had something important to attend to then, yet determined not to hurry or not to turn to the next thing until his present one was done. Watching him, Father Shay felt a queer and unexpected reassurance—the old man looked so busy, so purposive, sitting there praying. Father Shay began to pray in his own mind, rather unsteadily, for strength and for guidance. Just then Father Lordy snapped his breviary shut. "Now!" he said. He laid the book on the couch beside him.

Father Shay cleared his throat. "I—I have something to tell you, Father. Something that happened—" He broke off; he didn't know exactly how to tell it.

"Well, I have something to tell you first," Father Lordy said. He looked very pleased yet very severe, as if he were holding himself in with difficulty. "What you said after supper got me to thinking, you know. It really got me to thinking. You see, we've never had trouble like this in town before." He paused reminiscently; but almost at once he leaned forward, hands on his knees. "Well!" he said. "Anyhow, I left church early tonight, and I've been around seeing a few people—just little hurry-up calls, you know, but people who'll work with us on this thing. It's nothing revolutionary, you understand, nothing sensational right now—I'll tell you all about it—but it'll grow. We have to start things like this carefully if we don't want to make mistakes. There's a way to do things and a way not to do them. Now I'll tell you." Leaning forward he pointed one finger at Father Shay, and his voice grew almost conspiratorial—"We're *both* going to preach tomorrow, and afterward—"

But Father Shay couldn't follow the plans clearly just then. It was as it had been in the church earlier tonight, their footsteps sounding together: a sense of companionship, of being *with* someone. He felt the firm reserved strength of the old priest; and if he couldn't make out the words clearly, the voice itself was enough just then, it was what he most needed. In his relief, or beyond it, over it, a faint happiness stirred him; because in a way he was himself responsible, in a way he had started all this. As he sat there, staring at Father Lordy, he felt what seemed an ancient and far-away excitement rising warm and green within him for tomorrow.

LEAVING THE CHURCH
by Mark Helprin

"I HAVE never been as calm in my life," said Father Trelew. "No, not ever." He was speaking to Helen, his housekeeper, but she was not much in his mind, even though she had been with him for several years—he could not remember exactly how many. He looked at the sky. "Soon I will be on the plane to New York, and then to Rome."

"Have you been to Rome before, Father?"

"Yes, I have, in 1925 when Mussolini was in power. You know what I think of him, don't you, don't you, Helen."

"I most certainly do."

It was hot where they stood, but his clothes were clean and white and his thick hair was white, so he had no discomfort. There was a black spot of oil on the drive. A shimmering desert stretched beyond—his parish. He could smell the hot sand and see waves of heat rising from it, distorting the mountains.

The driver put his bags in the car, and after bidding goodbye to Helen and shaking her hand Father Trelew got in the back and clicked the door shut. The car was air-conditioned. It was taking him to Phoenix for the plane. He was going to Vatican II.

It was years since he had left his parish. In

New York before his parents died, they had called him sometimes "The Indian Priest," but he never heard them, they thought. They were ashamed of him. The wanted him to be an archbishop. Instead he spoke to deep-brown faces in a dark church with no lighting, while the sand blew outside. He could see it through the window sometimes—perfectly white against the blue sky and billowing like foam on the ocean, and yet it was cool and dry. His mother and father thought he would come back from Arizona as if from some foreign campaign, distinguished and likely to advance. The bishops would appreciate his sacrifice. He knew he was not coming back, but he never told his parents. They died in the Depression, sure that at the end of the Depression he would be called back from Arizona.

If he thought about being an archbishop, he clenched his fist and banged it on the table. When he had too much to drink, he thought wild thoughts about seeing God, about golden staircases and whitened plumes rising from the wide floor of Heaven, about places where it was so bright you couldn't see anything at all. He had such prideful dreams only after wine or whiskey, so he drank rarely.

He arrived in Rome early in the morning. He felt young, for he had slept on the plane and Rome seemed to him not to have changed since 1925, when he was thirty and had been there for two months as a student. Now there were few carriages, but the streets were the same. In Piazza Navona, the old colors still stood; the fountains had been going for almost forty years since he first saw them. He wondered if they ever stopped, for even a moment. Perhaps each time the city died—after the March, or when the Germans were there—the fountains stopped. He thought to ask an old man, but realized that no one man would have watched constantly, and besides, he thought, I am an old man and could tell no one if ever in Arizona the mountains turned pure white or the sky the color of gold, because I have not watched them the whole time. At least, the fountains appear never to stop; at least, I have seen them while they were going.

His budget for this trip was delightfully large. The Vatican paid much of it, his diocese another great part, and his savings the rest. He thought he would live for this short time in a fashion unlike that of his small frame house on the reservation. There the wind came in a steady stream through an unputtied crack of the window. In the morning gold light glinted off his porcelain shaving basin. At these times there was only silence and cold. After he shaved, he opened the window, and after he opened the window he dressed and prayed—but not in Rome. He would pray, yes, but in Rome he would pray in his own good time. There would be no kneeling on hard wooden floors, no fasting, and no cold.

He checked in at the Grand Hotel, which was full of priests and extremely elegant—marble, rich Oriental rugs, chandeliers, and in his room French doors with a view of a piazza and its enormous fountain shooting a hundred feet upward. As the weeks passed, he habitually ate his breakfast on the balcony. With high winds, he felt slight droplets of spray from the fountain. His bed was large, with a satin quilt. As always when he stayed in hotels—even in Phoenix—he wondered what people had made love in the bed, and then laughed good-naturedly at himself. He had learned to live with *that* a long time ago.

Father Trelew's role at the Council was not very exciting; indeed, the Council itself was not very exciting. He was just a priest. From where he sat near the entrance of St. Peter's, the Pope was only a white spot and the Dove of the Holy Ghost a needlepoint of light—a ray. When he removed his glasses, the sea of cardinals before the Pope was a mass of red, and when they stood their motion made them look like red waves. They were seated on both sides of the aisle. It was as if Moses had spread them back into the galleries. But whom would Father Trelew tell? Helen? Helen thought only of her child, who broke windows and stayed alone in the hills at night even when it was cold. Perhaps Father

Wohlen from Los Angeles, who was Father Trelew's friend simply because they were both at the Grand Hotel; Father Wohlen had an idea that anyone from west of the Mississippi was somehow a loving brother. But Father Trelew did not like Father Wohlen, for he ate too much and had an unconvincing laugh. There was no one to tell. "There is no one to tell," he said. "Maybe I will sketch it." He had not sketched since he had last been in Rome. He was in a drawing class then. He was mainly interested in architectural form; Rome offered him that, while the desert did not. He had tried to paint the Indians and the things they did, but there was not much left of them by that time, and he suspected not much left of him—or, rather, of his talent to draw.

Did he dare begin again? "I must," he said, the blood coursing to his face. The hair at his temples was silver. When his face lit up, he looked like giltwork. I am the only priest in the world, he thought, who looks like a church. He would have to buy a pad and charcoal.

One day, he left the council early and began the walk back to his hotel. He passed through Piazza Navona, and somewhere off it on a side street he found an art store. "Could I have," he began but found that he was not able to speak the words. "Could I have..." and then, like a madman, he rushed from the shop.

He was disturbed by this, knowing precisely what it was. He tried not to think, flooding his mind with words that formed in silence on his lips, like the cries of men in dreams of sinking ships. "Flood it with good cheer. Fill it up, fill it up, for life is short." If he could somehow get supplies, he could sit by the fountain and sketch.

What is the power of a priest's life? It is that he need not fear. "Father Wohlen," he said next day, too nervously, "do you think that on the way back from the Cathedral tomorrow you could stop in an art shop and get me a large pad and some charcoal?" He gasped for breath. "Because I must stay late for chapel vespers. I don't mean to trouble you..."

"No trouble, no trouble," said Father Wohlen. "I'll do it. You just give me the money, tell me where to go, and I'll do it."

Father Trelew did not go to vespers; he did not even go to the Council that day. It was an important day, too. He stayed in his room, and it seemed to him that God was working wonders with his body. If he had been a proud man, he might have presumed that he was undergoing Divine revelation, that he was receiving saintly visions. Only once in his life, only once, had the rest of his body responded to his mind and made him tremble. No, it was the body responding to the *heart* which caused trembling.

He sat on the edge of his bed, with his glasses

off, and the blur of outside sunlight made him feel the enlivened world. "Oh my God, my dear God," he prayed, "I am not having visions, am I?" He said this to a shaft of sunlight in his room at his feet, and the golden dust danced in center beam.

When Father Wohlen gave him his materials, Father Wohlen thought Trelew was sick. Something was wrong with the man.

Father Trelew ran his hands over the pad, took the charcoal out of its box, and felt the smooth rectangular blocks. The cool of the blocks reminded him of the desert at evening, their blackness of the night, but the night was full of white stars. That was an advantage he would not have had as an archbishop—seeing the Milky Way stretched as a shimmering band over the great dome of his little life. The power of a priest's life is that he is unafraid. All is concelebration. "I am beginning to realize this," said Father Trelew. "That all is concelebration—all of the city, all of the stars. The Church is for me. A man need not fear his loneliness. He need not fear his loneliness, for God is strong and all is concelebration. The power of a priest's life is that he need not fear."

The next day he was up very early. He read most of *La Stampa.* A bus took him to the Vatican.

It would not be right for him to sketch in the

Cathedral. His idea was to study a particular scene and commit it to memory for drawing. Back in Arizona, he would paint it. Somehow he got very close to the Pope. Though it was thrilling to see him, it was not the Pope he chose to study but the under-secretaries close to the Papal Throne, seated at a table next to the balustrade of the Confessio.

Another priest from America was determined to guide him. "That is Bishop Wilhelm Kempf of Limburg," he said, "and Archbishop Villot of Lyons, Archbishop Krol of Philadelphia, and the archbishop of Madrid—I do not know his name."

"Thank you, thank you," said Father Trelew to the other priest, who wanted to say more, and then to escape he stepped much closer to the scene than he would ordinarily have dared. He was the foremost of observers; between him and the under-secretaries was only a slight and terrible plain of marble. The Pope was not far. I am so near greatness, he thought. Princes! He studied the scene. He had always had a good architectural memory. He was fine on detail, but here he was impressed by grandeur, which was glowing, descript, calling out to any man.

Entrenched in the blackness of distant high walls, the red table of the under-secretaries glowed scarlet; ringed with gold and tasselled, its colors moved in front of the eyes. The under-secretaries, in pure white with upswinging conical hats of flattened design, did not rest upon their red ribbons banded about them in curves and sweeps like water falling. They worked at papers, and they were in different positions, so that the tall conical hats pointed together in a smooth indication, like a crest of ocean foam, to the Pope. And beyond them was a swirling black column edged with a rotating blade of gold. It was so bright it made Father Trelew shudder. He stood for a good half hour, intent upon the secretaries. His gaze was powerful. He was having the time of his life, for he knew he would soon begin to draw.

One of the Papal secretaries noticed Father Trelew when he first came, and then again after half an hour. He thought perhaps he was wanted and crossed the forbidden marble at a glide. His robes were such that his feet did not seem to move. "Is there anything I can do for you, Father?" he said curiously.

Father Trelew, who had tried and failed to escape when he saw the bishop coming, could not answer. His steadfastness had provoked the great man, but he could not answer. His mouth hung open.

"Are you all right?" the bishop asked. He laughed pleasantly and touched Father Trelew, who felt again like sinking ships, and whose mouth was still open while the bishop returned to his table, silent and smiling.

Father Trelew managed to close his mouth as he walked back into the crowd. Everyone looked at him as if he were in some way connected to the Pope. He might have enjoyed that had he been able to answer the bishop, but he was expressionless and numb. And yet he did not panic. He wanted to get back to the hotel to draw, and then the next day to Piazza Navona, with his pad, to sketch the central fountain. He could use his material freely there. He was marvellously excited. He quickly forgot the incident with the bishop, bent down to tie his shoe, and strode like a master through St. Peter's to home in the hotel. He did not think, Oh, I am such a little man, until he arrived in his room and could not draw what he had remembered.

Father Trelew had many times told weeping Indian women that sleep helped the troubled. He had many times watched tears travel down a face like wind-cut brown granite—sparkling black eyes in the church's dimness—and thought how deeply the woman would sleep. Always the next day he saw her going about her business, which is precisely what *he* did the next day.

Late in the afternoon, he found himself in Piazza Navona. He thought to draw the fountain and the buildings vanishing in perspective, to test his draftsmanship. He planned to have dinner at one of the restaurants there so popular with Roman families (fairly well-to-do, he assumed) and clerics, and perhaps find an acquaintance with whom to chat as it got dark.

He took a seat at one of the smaller fountains and put his legs up on the stone wall. In his freshly pressed white suit he looked as if he might have been a missionary from the Congo or Asia. "Perhaps they think I am a jungle priest," he said happily. "But I am not a jungle priest, I am a desert priest—and how many of those are there? Very few in the Sahara, none, as far as I know, in the Gobi, and none in the Nafud. That leaves me, and a few others. I should find out who they are, write to them, perhaps start a journal."

He was a good priest, and did his job well. He thought of photographers he had seen on the reservation, who paid people small sums to be photographed and recorded their humiliation and discomfort only to pass it off to the world as the pathos of humankind. In the operations of caring for his flock, Father Trelew tried to avoid the photographer's fallacy. Only rarely did tragedy face them. There were complaints and sorrows, but not much passionate loss. He had to accept that. It was a small population, and not a battlefield—he was *truly* needed once in a great while, but he refused to buy the illusion that when they came to him aching from life in the world he was doing great service. In that way, when he did great service he felt he could vault over mountains. In other words, he was a lean man.

He thought, My dreams can be dreamed in forty-five minutes, and then I become either tired or empty and stop dreaming—again, leanness. In the weakening sun he began to sketch Piazza Navona, and his hand moved rapidly, surprising him with what it had remembered. He included cars and carriages, and the horses, drawn well. After several hours, when it was dark, he closed his pad and put a little piece of charcoal into the box, which he then put in his pocket. Putting the box in his pocket was like the sheriff putting his gun back in his holster after a shoot-out. When he swung his legs back to the ground it was as if they had boots and spurs. He had drawn the Piazza, and it was therefore his.

With dinner, he ordered a bottle of white wine. He was not used to it; it was a mistake, he told himself halfway through, but drank it anyway. Then everything began to fall into place as he watched the lights of Rome in the heat of September and wandered about like a young drunk.

He was a good-natured man, had always been a good-natured man. His father, who was ambitious for him to the point of hating him, said once, "Michael, what have you got, what the hell have you got?" Father Trelew had wanted to reply that he was a good man, could draw, and loved God. But he wept instead, and only later, half weeping, did he say to his mother, "Tell him, by my honor, that I am just a man," and left for the train to the West.

He was good-looking. He had a wonderful face. Even at his age, and he was almost seventy, women were not unmoved by his glance. When he was younger they had frequently fallen in love with him, especially the troubled ones, who always fall for priests of one sort or another. There had been one in Rome in 1925, when he was thirty and had rebuffed already a good many trouble-seekers and those testing their power. A priest is familair with that. He can handle that. It is the guileless ones, the ones who really love, who make things difficult.

In 1925, the library of the old Accademia was farmed with sea-green reader's lamps, which glowed in the day. The walls were so old one might have been sorry for them had they not been painted with angels, gardens, and bursting suns.

Father Trelew was not merely appreciative but ecstatic. He often stayed in the library all day and well into the evening. He was writing a paper on Oderisi da Gubbio, a miniaturist of the thirteenth century. When he left the library he saw only the colors he had seen all day in illuminated manuscripts. It seemed to him that he sailed home without a word, simply gliding and brimming.

One was assigned a seat, and results were not always pleasing. Harvard undergraduates dying for the sunburnt girl in purple who sometimes wore black were placed across the room from her facing the other way into a bunch of nuns. Father Trelew could hardly breathe for two weeks; he was the only man at a table for Radcliffe girls. One of them fell in love with him, just by looking.

"What is your name...Father?" she asked, since there was no one else at the table.

"Michael Trelew," he said frightenedly.

"And where are you from?"

"From. From. I'm from Ossining, New York. Perhaps you have heard of us—I mean it, as it is the home of Sing Sing Prison. Where are you from?"

"Forty-nine East Eighty-sixth Street," she said, waiting.

His fear was beginning to bore him, and in anger he wanted to be reckless, if only not to be dull. But he could only stare at her. She was thin, and blond. He could not decide if she looked like the Madonna. She was very brown and her dress was white.

She said, and with her green eyes, "Can we eat

together tonight?" It was for her a difficult request, and she blushed. She felt like what she thought of popular music—brash but finally very beautiful. She was embarrassed by her own directness, expectant, and altogether very open and tender.

Father Trelew was taken. Yet he answered as if from a prepared hollowness, "I have no money. I am a priest..." He hesitated, because he was no longer interested in what he was saying. Instead, visions of neutral Switzerland flashed at him and he entertained the profoundly impossible notion of running away with this girl.

The weeks that followed were very sad for both of them. They were both gaining, but they were also losing, and perhaps what united them so strongly at first was that they felt they knew what the other was relinquishing. And then they had that particular camaraderie which exists among schoolboys, soldiers, and outlaws.

It did not take long before they were speeding to Switzerland in a touring car he had rented with the remainder of his grant for study in Rome. He told her the speedometer's thin red needle reminded him of a hummingbird's tongue. They stopped at a dam in a valley of the Alps. Across the spillway was an automobile bridge that led nowhere, and fog from the rushing water cascaded in a convection arch over the bridge, over the two of them.

The time together in Rome had made the priest and the girl heady. She was young, and he not so young but it was new to him. When he removed his collar he sighed in relief and walked out into the warm sun where she was waiting in the open car in a hat and heavy coat ready to head north. There was singing all the way. In one inn, Father Trelew, having had too much wine, told the porter that he was a priest. The porter raised his arms as if to say, "That is very serious, but so what?"

They stayed in Switzerland for more than a month. He was going to give up the Church, when she left him. There was no comfort. Everything had failed. He had not written his paper and could show nothing for his summer in Italy. The bishops at home would have his head for that. There would be nothing he could say; he could see himself gaping at them.

It would not be the first time he had found himself mute. The first was the time he and the girl had been unable to resolve an argument and it grew wider and wider, until she was on a platform waiting for a train and nothing he could say made anything better. He felt untrained for that sort of thing. The argument had started while they were drawing by a lake, and he threw his picture to the ground. He was angry. She had too many plans for him. She had him in the White House when he was not yet even just a defrocked priest. He threw his picture on the ground because he realized that she was young and nothing could be done about it. When the train came, she was crying, for she did love him, and perhaps because she was crying and she was young she struck a blow she had not meant to strike. She was not even Catholic but Episcopalian. She said through the steam and rain which soaked them both and was warm and very much like their tears—she said on that hot misty August day so uncommon for Switzerland, "And you are such a little man." It was then that his mouth dropped open and he could say nothing. She cried and cried, and as the train left he ran after it halfheartedly with his mouth still open and tears streaming down his cheeks and the steam from the gaskets making his suit smell as if it had been just pressed.

He looked at the high white mountains, and his smallness choked him. He boarded the next train to Rome after waiting in the station for seventeen hours. He did not eat, nor did he return for his belongings. It stayed misty and warm until he left.

They sent him to Arizona. They would have thrown him out, but they needed someone there. He was perfect for the job. He could have left on his own. They offered him that, but he was afraid. The archbishop made him afraid. Offices made him afraid. Even cathedrals now made him afraid.

The only thing that calmed him was the desert

and its silent, dry heat. In the desert he started to seek God as he had not ever sought him. In some ways he stayed weak, and in others he became very strong.

He watched the blue mountains and the billowing sand, which was like the foam on the ocean when he came home from Italy, but cool and dry.

A man from the desert is not a dry man, but he keeps what is wet inside him, like a cactus, so that visitors to him wonder how in such a world he can be alive and have enough. Father Trelew had not been born in the desert, but his forty years there taught him much. Although there will be some who might deny that a man may be taught such a thing, it is a fact that Father Trelew was calm, quiet, and gracious during his first heart attack. It occurred while he dined with several other American priests near the hotel in a restaurant they had all frequented during the first weeks of the Council, and then abandoned, then remembered and rushed to, as Father Trelew had done with his drawing. He ate prosciutto and melon, *scaloppine alla zingara*, and drank gaseous mineral water and cold white wine. He was contemplating dessert and had his wine-glass raised to his lips when he felt the first pain. It seemed as if the entire restaurant had been jolted by an earthquake, and the electricity somehow savagely unleashed to attack the assembled priests. At first he thought there *had* been an earthquake. He kept his glass to his lips, afraid to move. He would put it down, slowly. He would go without dessert, excuse himself, and walk to see a doctor. He did not want to trouble his companions, because they were younger and he felt they did not like him; he had said hardly a thing in the course of the meal while they burned with the politics of Council.

But he could not move his arm to put his glass down. It was there for a full minute and no one noticed until he fell to the ground, for he could not stand the second wave. He fell to the ground still with the glass in his hand, apologizing and begging the pardon of the assembled priests, who were younger and who had ignored him.

When he awakened in his hospital room, he was grateful that the walls were not white. Rome is a yellow color, an old saffron-powdered sun color which seems always rising upward. His room was a comforting beige, the color of a lightly done roll in the oven.

He was happy to be alive and would not move his head until later, when a nun told him it was safe. He saw by turning his eyes the tops of pine trees and green hills in the not so far distance. He judged himself to be on a mountaintop. "Splendid," he said. "I'm on a mountaintop." He could hear birds and the clicking of crutches in the garden. After a few weeks he was up and about. He could see most of Rome from the garden and some of Rome came up to meet him, although that part of Rome which travelled up the hillside to him was not people but houses and streets.

When he had been a priest in Arizona and visited parishioners in the hospital he thought because of its bustle and crowded corridors that a hospital was a social place. He had often thought of going to a hospital on some physical excuse to cure his loneliness, but in Rome (and he assumed that hospitals were spiritually the same everywhere) he discovered himself more alone than he had ever been. The face of his nurse was constantly changing, and there were eight doctors who cared for him in varying degree, none with particular intensity. He was alone during the day, and in the night. He did not dare draw. He was afraid to look in the mirror. No one paid him any attention, because he was old.

There was a man dying of some unknown disease, a violinist in a symphony orchestra in the North of Italy. He looked as if he were made of old loops and patches. He smelled of death. It came from inside him—from his bowels, from his throat, even from his legs and fingers. Father Trelew had smelled the same smell in Arizona when some boys cut open a deer they had shot in the mountains several days before. Every day the violinist sat in the garden and played. He was particularly fond of the Andante of Prokofieff's Second Violin Concerto, and he played it again and again. The officials allowed it because it helped those who recovered recover, those who were dying to die, and those in the middle of the road to pass the time. Father Trelew wanted to talk to the man whose music was so beautiful; he had never before heard any Prokofieff. When he went to him in the garden, he found the old man unable to speak. But the patterns of the music were so strongly ingrained, and his hands so powerful, that he played, he played, until the day of his death—not always correctly, often out of time, but always with much passion.

Father Trelew was not afraid of dying. He was afraid of what he might be before he died. When he first realized that he was dying he stayed in his chair—an old man in a chair—and tried frantically to remember all the parts of his life. He thought that when a man dies a man reviews what he has seen. He expected memories to jolt his frame, and visions to seek him and turn him, and shower the room with light.

But it just didn't happen as he expected, which he might have expected but did not. He became whimsical, prided himself suddenly on his sense of humor, and found the truth in sayings. He would say, "Love makes the world go round," and laugh. He was generally good-natured.

Every four hours a nurse, never the same one, came to ask him if he had moved his bowels. He thought this was hilarious.

"Father Trelew."

"Yes, Sister."

"Have you moved your bowels in the last four hours?"

"Moved them where?" he said, and burst out laughing.

He was happy for no particular reason, and for that reason he adjudged himself particularly happy. One would have thought he was getting better. He said, "I want to have a good time on earth while I can," and spent the days in the garden, in the sun, watching flowers and delighting in the smell of rich grass, which was green as if on a riverbank. At night, he looked from his window at Rome, and because he remembered his memories so well he did not think of them, or need to. One look at Rome from a moderate distance was to see his life, but it was past and he had no need for that.

A week after the death of the violinist who could not speak, Father Trelew died. The bishops of New York sent a militant priest who had been embarrassing them to fill his place in Arizona. He died in late afternoon. It had been raining. He knew from years before in his student days that there is a special name for raindrops in Rome because they are often so big, but he could not remember it. He was admiring the light coming off the wet buildings, and he was calm, listening to the wash of the rain. The bushes in the garden glistened with drops, and when someone went by and hit them the water flew off like water off a vibrating dog. Streams of warm water coursed down the gray stone streets of the mountain—or hill—of the hospital. All across Rome flocks of pigeons were seeking the rays of sun, which came from holes in the clouds, and they flew in great masses, looking for light that quickly vanished with new configurations of the dark sky. Father Trelew listened to the work of the rain, to the wash of the rain, and to a car going through a puddle. The water is warm, the blood of the earth. He was a man resting for the afternoon in his chair. Warm breezes thick with invisible mist moved his white gauze curtains, and he faced the wind. He turned his head to it and breathed it in.

Then it seemed again as if there were an earthquake. For an instant he imagined that lightning had hit him, for his vision had flashed white at first, but then he knew, and when the bolts kept on coming he knew he was dying and he became very excited.

He tried to think of the girl he had once loved—of her face, of the heat and their well-being—but could not do it. He had not enough time. He realized that dying takes away time, and that is all, and he was dying when fear gripped him and his mouth dropped open in its customary manner. He had planned to die with a vision, but there was no vision. The rain had stopped, and the water ceased to flow as rapidly inside the gutters. He noticed that. The walls seemed to him a very dark olive-green instead of tan. His mouth hung open, but he raised himself in his chair of a sudden and said, "Damn you, shut, damn it!" and it did shut and he was so surprised that he smiled and his eyes came alive. It seemed to him that he was a new man, that he was no longer a priest, no longer Michael Trelew. He was only sorry that they would bury him as Michael Trelew, Priest. He had gone out of those doors.

He lived that way for the short span of time between the lighting of his eyes and the entrance of a priest who was rushing in the door to administer last rites. Father Trelew saw the priest through the corner of his eye, but by the time he would have had full view he was dead. The last thing he thought was how beautiful the summer rain in Rome—and he died, and he died with great courage.

VANITY
by Frank O'Connor

THERE are a lot of things old bishops have to put up with besides old age, loneliness, and lack of domestic comforts, and the worst of these is coadjutors. To be God Almighty—the just and moral Governor of the universe—for years and years, and then have an assistant God Almighty tagged on you to see that your justice and morality are of the proper kind, is a more than human ordeal. The Bishop of Moyle, the Most Reverent Dr. Gallogly, called his coadjutor the Stump, the Spy, or the Boy, according to the way he felt about him. Mostly the Boy. The Boy had nasty supercilious ways that the Bishop detested. He let on to know a lot about French history, gave himself out for an authority on food and wine, jeered at Dr. Gallogly's coffee—the best bottled coffee on the market—and mocked at Dr. Gallogly's statement that the best food and wine in the world were to be had on the train from Holyhead to Euston. It must be admitted that the Bishop was vulnerable to that sort of criticism. As a one-time Professor of Dogmatic Theology he tended to turn everything into a dogma.

What was worse than that, the coadjutor was a bit of a snob, and what was worst of all, he had the illusion that at eighty-six the Bishop was past his prime, whereas the Bishop knew well that he had never been brighter in his wits. Just to show Lanigan, he would suddenly order round the car, drive a couple of hundred miles to Dublin, stay at the best hotel, interview three Ministers and ask them all about their Departments, and then come home and tell Lanigan nothing. Lanigan let on to be amused at this as just another example of the old Bishop's irresponsibility, but, being an inquisitive man himself, the Bishop knew he was mad at not knowing what went on, and only pretended not to care out of vanity. Vanity—the besetting sin of people in religion, according to Dr. Gallogly—was Lanigan's as well, and at heart the Bishop knew he was wild.

Whenever the notion of going to Dublin struck the Bishop, he always made inquiries about people from Moyle who might be staying there, so that he could call. He knew they liked that; it was a thing they could brag about, and afterwards they came back and said what a wonderful old man he was—another thorn in Lanigan's flesh.

One morning before he set out, he discovered that one of his curates was in a nursing home in Dublin for a major operation.

"Father O'Brien?" he exclaimed in astonishment. "What's he doing with an operation. Sure, he's only—what is he, father?"

"Forty-five, my Lord."

"Forty-five! And having operations! Sure, there's no sense in that. Remind me to go and see

Father O'Brien, Paddy,'' he added to his chauffeur.

Even the Bishop's best friend wouldn't have pretended that this was pure kindness, though he had plenty of that. It was mainly wonder at himself, having reached the age of eighty-six without a surgeon's ever sticking a knife in him, while a whole generation of priests was growing up that couldn't even reach forty-five without an operation of some sort. Motor-cars! It couldn't be anything else only motor-cars.

And every step he climbed up to the first-floor room of the nursing home, the Bishop vacillated between good nature and complacency; good nature in being able to do a good turn for a lonesome young priest, far from his friends and family, and a furious complacency that it wasn't the young fellow of forty-five who was coming to visit the old man, but the fine, upstanding old man of eighty-six who was coming to visit the young fellow. And the two emotions mingled in the triumphant smile with which he opened the young priest's door and trumpeted joyously ''Father O'Brien, do you want me to suspend you? Wouldn't you get up out of that and attend to your duties?'' That would get back to Lanigan as well.

What at home might have been an ordeal for the curate became, because of the unfamiliar surroundings and the Bishop's excitement, a most enjoyable occasion for both. The Bishop was no fool, but because he was behaving rather foolishly, he talked with more freedom than he would otherwise have permitted himself about the Moyle clergy and their families. A bishop has to know everything, and he realized that you could never know a man unless you knew his family. You could never explain the extraordinary behaviour of a man like Lanigan unless you knew about his brother, the parish priest, who not only had died young of a particularly wishy-washy disease that would never have killed anyone else but had suffered for two years before he died from scruples. Scruples!

"Nerves!" said the Bishop. "All that family were neurotic. You'll see, he'll go just the same way."

He returned to his hotel, saying to Paddy, his "man": "That'll show them, Paddy," and Paddy grinned because he knew well whom the Bishop was referring to. There is nobody who resents a coadjutor more than a Bishop's man. The lounge of the hotel was crowded and several people were waiting for the lift, but by this time the Bishop's complacency was contemptuous of every obstacle. "Ah, I can't be bothered waiting for that machine," he said, loud enough to be overheard by everyone; and went up the stairs "like a hare," as Paddy put it, though this was really comparison gone mad.

He negotiated the main stair successfully, but when he came to a flight of six steps leading disconcertingly from one level to another, he slipped. He had only six steps to fall, but he knew they might as well have been twenty. He was dished. He didn't move; he knew it wasn't safe. "Pride goeth before a fall," he thought. "I should have waited for that blooming old lift."

"I think I'm hurt," he said to the waiter who rushed to his aid. "Don't tell anyone. Get something to lift me in on and call Dr. Jameson."

It was agony being transferred to the stretcher and from the stretcher to the bed, but pain was the least of the Bishop's troubles, and the tears in his blue eyes were as much humiliation as anything else. After an irreproachable life of eighty-six years he was suddenly, because of what he now called "a mad vagary," no longer his own master, and as much subject to stretcher-bearers, doctors, and nurses as any poor curate. Lanigan's opportunity had come. No longer would they talk of him in Moyle as a wonderful old man. The shock of it was almost enough to make him lose his reason.

"Am I bad?" he asked the doctor bleakly.

"It looks as if you've broken your shoulder and leg," said the doctor, a brisk, moon-faced young man. "We'll have to get you to hospital and see if there's anything else."

"Am I going to die?" asked the Bishop almost hopefully. If he were really going to die, there would be no further problem.

"You must be pretty tough to have reached your age," said the doctor, who was privately convinced that the Bishop wouldn't leave the hospital outside a box.

"Ah, I'm tough enough," said the Bishop. "Couldn't you do whatever you have to do here?"

"I could not," said the doctor in alarm.

"Why couldn't you?" asked the Bishop angrily. He hated to be contradicted in that positive way—it is one of the drawbacks of having been Almighty God.

"Because I have to get an X-ray at once."

"Couldn't you get it here? I'm a busy man. I haven't the time for going to hospital."

"But you have to go to hospital."

"If you were in my position, you'd see why I don't want to go to hospital," the Bishop said earnestly. "People think when a man has authority that he can do as he likes. He can't. He always has people after him, trying to make out he's not fit to look after himself. They want to treat you as if you were a child. If this gets round, it's going to be very awkward for me."

"But an accident can happen to anybody," protested the doctor.

"An accident can happen to a young man,"

the Bishop said, wincing. "What happens to an old man isn't supposed to be an accident. You'd think, the way they go on, that we did it out of spite. The manager here is an old friend of mine. I can trust him to keep his mind to himself."

"You're asking for impossibilities," the doctor said. "You needn't be worried about the nursing home. You'll be as comfortable there as you are here."

"I don't give a rap about comfort," said the Bishop with an indignant flash of his blue eyes. "But if I go into a nursing home, 'twill be all round Moyle by tomorrow."

"It'll be all round Moyle anyway."

"It will not be all round Moyle if I can prevent it."

"But people will have to know."

"Why will they have to know?" the Bishop asked fiercely. It was bad enough to be enduring that pain and worse to be enduring complete helplessness, without being contradicted into the bargain. "What business is it of anyone's?" Then, as his mind began again to play with the possibilities, his voice grew milder. "Supposing I do go to hospital, can't I go under a false name?"

"But you'd have to tell the nuns," said the doctor aghast.

"I would *not* tell the nuns," the Bishop said with renewed irascibility. "You don't know what you're talking about. I know more about nuns than you do, and I wouldn't tell a nun anything."

"But they'd have to know you were a clergyman."

"I tell you you don't know what you're talking about, man. A clergyman in this country has no privacy. The first thing they'd want to know was what diocese I was from, and then there would be a nun or a nurse with a brother a priest in the same diocese. As a matter of fact, there's a curate there from my own diocese. There's too much curiosity about priests in this country."

"Let me give you something to ease that pain before you talk any more," said the doctor, seeing that the Bishop was on the point of collapse.

"I'm not going to be taking any drugs from you till I know where I stand," said the Bishop. "What sort of woman is the Reverend Mother in that place?"

"She's a nice, friendly woman."

"Never mind how friendly she is. Where is she from?"

"I never asked her."

"And isn't it a great wonder you wouldn't find out?" said the Bishop, who knew that if only he knew her father or her brother, he could guess how reliable she was. "Is she young or old?"

"Oldish."

"Ask her to come here and talk to me."

"Do you know, my Lord, you're a very obstinate old man?" said the doctor.

"Ah, if you had my responsibilities, you'd be the same," grunted the Bishop without rancour. He liked to be told he was obstinate. It showed that he was a man who knew his own mind. "Bring her here to me and I'll talk to her myself."

Ten minutes later the doctor returned with the nun. She was an oldish, soft-mannered, gigglesome woman who almost smothered the Bishop with her solicitude. He let her moan on, knowing it was only part of her stock in trade, and waited till the doctor left the room before putting his hand on hers.

"The doctor is a very bright young man, mother," he said earnestly, "but he's not easy to talk to. 'Tisn't often you'll find a layman that can understand the difficulties of people in religion."

"Sure, how could he?" she asked.

"And the reason is," he said solemnly, "that every calling has its own graces and temptations. Now, the great temptation of religious people is vanity."

"I wonder, my Lord," she said coyly, as if she had noticed a few others.

"You needn't," replied the Bishop in the tone he used for proclaiming the merits of the Holyhead train. "That is what makes it so hard for people in religion to be growing old. You're a young woman yet," he went on with brazen flattery, "so you wouldn't know."

"Oh, indeed, I'm afraid, so far as that goes, I'm older than you give me credit for," she said, growing alarmingly girlish.

"Why then, indeed, you are not," said the Bishop confidently, knowing that he had won her ear. "But your own turn will come. You'll see the young people pushing you to make way for them, watching you and criticizing you; waiting for you to make a slip."

"Ah, indeed, my Lord, I've seen it already."

"I can see you're an understanding woman," said the Bishop solemnly. "Now, mother, this is a thing I could not say to a lay person, but I can say it to you. I have a coadjutor, and we do not get on. I know this won't go any further. That young man takes too much on himself. He thinks I'm not fit to look after myself. If he knows I had an accident, it will give him a hold over me. He will say I am not fit to be taking decisions on my own. I do not like to be criticizing, but there is nothing he is not vain enough to think."

"My Lord," she said in alarm, "I don't think you know what you're asking."

"Mother," he said compellingly, "there is nothing an intelligent woman cannot do, if she puts her mind to it."

"My Lord," she said, "there is nothing an

inquisitive woman can't find out if she puts her mind to it."

However, she gave her word to do her best. There had been, she admitted, certain private patients whose identity had had to be concealed for reasons of policy, and some distinguished patients whose delirium tremens had to be disguised as something else. She would do what she could. That evening the Bishop was comfortably settled in a room corridors away from the rest of the nursing home, with two old nuns to look after him. The old nuns had long ceased to be active; one of them was crippled with rheumatics and the other slightly gone in the head, but they rejoiced in their responsibility, exulted in the fact that at last they had been found indispensable, revenged themselves on those who had slighted their age and infirmity by a scornful silence, and guarded the Bishop with something approaching ferocity.

The Bishop was in great pain, but even the pain didn't hinder his feeling of complacency. He had arranged everything. The curate was in the same nursing home, and was probably lying awake marvelling at the Bishop's sturdy health, while all the time the Bishop was lying near him, as helpless as himself, but content in the feeling that what Father O'Brien didn't know wouldn't harm him. The essence of authority consists in keeping your secrets.

But after the first day or two even the Bishop became aware of the atmosphere of mystery in which Reverend Mother had wrapped him. She was the only other nun permitted to visit him. The nurses weren't allowed into his room at all. But the trouble with the Bishop's gallant old watch-dogs was that they had lost their teeth. They were easy game for the younger nuns and the nurses, because Sister Martha's bad head and Sister Dympna's bad legs meant that when they left his room there was no guarantee that they would ever get back. On the third day the door suddenly opened and a middle-aged, scraggy-looking nurse came in and looked at him in apparent astonishment.

"I'm sorry," she said, giving him a crooked smile. "Are you Mr. Murphy?"

"No," said the Bishop with a glare. "I'm Mr. Dempsey."

"You wouldn't be one of the Dempseys from Limerick?" she asked. "The motor people?"

"No," he replied brazenly. "My family came from Kanturk."

"We had a nurse one time from Kanturk," she said, screwing up her eyes. "Lucey, her name was. You wouldn't know her?"

"She must be from another part of Kanturk," said the Bishop.

"I dare say," she said, realizing that she had met her match. "From the other side of the post office. What happened you anyway?"

"A fall I got off my bicycle," said the Bishop.

An inquisitive man himself, the Bishop deeply resented inquisitiveness, and he had never met inquisitiveness to match that of the nurse. For a while after she left the room he was boiling with rage and decided that it was almost a matter for a pastoral letter. But as he thought of it, he realized that there was something about the nurse's air which he resented even more. The woman had been familiar with him. She had shown him no proper respect. As he thought of it his anger vanished and gave place to a feeling of his own guile. He realized now that Reverend Mother had really succeeded in baffling her staff, and that they thought he was probably a rich businessman or politician whose illness had to be concealed from his enemies. It impressed him that even as such he had been treated with such little ceremony. As a young priest he had noticed how conversation changed when he entered a room. Now, in his old age, he was getting the real thing—the tone people adopted among themselves. The religious life was too sheltered. As a result he never reported the visit of the nurse and even waited impatiently for her to come back.

In her place there came a young and good-looking girl who didn't even pretend to have strayed into his room by accident. She looked at him with a guilty air, and then her small, keen eyes started to wander, looking for a clue.

"They say you were in America; were you?" she asked.

"What makes them think that?" asked the Bishop.

"I don't know. I suppose because you don't seem to have any family here."

"Well, I'll tell you the truth, girl," the Bishop said slyly, "I haven't a family. I was never what you'd call a marrying man."

"Why would you?" she asked with a shrug. "I suppose you can get them without."

For a moment the Bishop was so stunned that he almost gave himself away. He looked at the young nurse again, but her pretty face still remained vague and sweet and innocent.

"Isn't that a shocking thing for a girl like you to say?" he asked indignantly.

"What's shocking about it?" she asked ingenuously. "I suppose you're not going to pretend you did without them?"

It left the Bishop very thoughtful. There were apparently lots of things that had escaped him even in his eighty-six years. "Too sheltered," he muttered to himself again. "Too blooming sheltered. We don't know the half that's going on. We might as well have blinkers." What surprised him most was that he was becoming almost attached to his anonymity, and grew quite hopeful when he heard a woman's step outside his door that it might be another of the nurses coming to pump him. When the first nurse returned to test a new theory of his identity and told him a dirty story, he wasn't even shocked. It had never occurred to him before that women knew dirty stories. "We live and learn," he thought.

Reverend Mother arranged his departure as she had arranged his arrival. The two old nuns knelt for his blessing, and had a little bawl because they would again be regarded as old and useless. One of them guarded the landing and another the hall while Paddy took down the bags. They passed the door of the curate's room. He was still there, poor fellow, though beginning to come round.

"I suppose you'll go straight to the hotel?" said the doctor.

"I will not," replied the Bishop. "I want to know what's going on in Moyle. That coadjutor of mine only waits till my back is turned."

"I can tell you now you're a very lucky man," said the doctor. "I thought you were for the long road. I have a patient of twenty-two that the same thing happened to, and he'll never walk again."

"Poor fellow! Poor fellow!" said the Bishop perfunctorily. "I suppose a lot of it is having the stamina."

He was bitterly disappointed on reaching Moyle to discover that everyone knew of his accident, but surprised at the warmth of his welcome. Crowds gathered and knelt for his blessing in the street, and the second day, when he called at Cronin's Hotel, he was cheered as he emerged. It puzzled him a lot. As a dogmatic theologian he never enthused himself, and he didn't understand other people's enthusing. It wouldn't have occurred to him that in a small town even the presence of two bishops was nearly as good a tonic as a boxing match.

"What the blazes ails them?" he asked Jerry Cronin.

"Ah, well, people were very upset when they heard of the accident," said Jerry in surprise.

"And I suppose they knew all about it within twenty-four hours?" said the Bishop indignantly.

"Oh, sooner than that, my Lord, sooner than that," said Jerry with a shocked air.

"Nuns! Nuns! Nuns!" muttered the Bishop. "You can never trust nuns."

THE PRESENCE OF GRACE

by J. F. Powers

ON a fine Sunday morning in June, Father Fabre opened the announcement book to familiarize himself with the names of the deceased in the parish for whom Masses would be offered in the coming week, and came upon a letter from the chancery office. The letter, dated December, dealt with the Legion of Decency pledge which should have been administered to the people at that time. Evidently Father Fabre was supposed to read it at the nine-thirty and eleven o'clock Masses that morning. He went to look for the pastor.

Father Fabre, ordained not quite a year, had his hands full at Trinity. It wasn't a well-run parish. The pastor was a hard man to interest in a problem. They saw each other at meals. Father Fabre had been inside the pastor's bedroom, the seat of all his inactivity, only once; Miss Burke, the housekeeper, never. The press of things was very great in the pastor's room, statues, candlesticks, cases of sacramental wine, bales of pious literature and outdated collection envelopes, two stray pews and a prie-dieu, the implements and furniture of his calling. There was a large table-model radio in his bed, and he obviously slept and made the bed around it. That was about it.

Father Fabre found the pastor in the dining room. "Little late for this, isn't it?" he said. He held out the letter which had wintered in the pastor's room.

"Don't watch me eat," said the pastor, a greying dormouse. He had had the six-thirty and eight o'clocks, and was breaking his fast—not very well, Father Fabre thought, still trying to see what was in the bowl. Shredded wheat *and* oatmeal? Something he'd made himself? Not necessarily. Miss Burke could make dishes like that.

The pastor shifted into a sidesaddle position, bending one of his narrow shoulders over the bowl, obstructing the curate's view.

Father Fabre considered the letter in his hand. . . . *immoral motion pictures/demoralizing television/indecent plays/vulgar radio programs/pernicious books/vicious papers and periodicals/degrading dance halls/and unwholesome taverns*. . . Was this the mind, the tongue of the Church? "Little late for this, isn't it?"

"No."

"I thought we were supposed to give it a long time ago." On the Sunday within the Octave of the Immaculate Conception, in fact. On that day, Trinity, pledgeless, had been unique among the churches of the diocese—so he'd bragged to friends, curates who were unhappy about the pledge, as he was, and he hadn't really blamed them for what they'd said out of envy, that it had been his duty to repair the ommission at his Masses. "Weren't we?"

"No."

"*No*?"

The dormouse shook his head a half inch. The spoon in his right hand was a precision instrument, scraping up the last of whatever had filled the bowl. Grain.

"I don't feel right about this," Father Fabre said, going away with the letter. He went to the sacristy to vest for the nine-thirty, talking to himself. It *was* a little late for the pledge. *No*. The Sunday within the Octave *had* been the day for it. *No*.

The white fiddleback chasuble he was putting on had been spoiled on Christmas. He'd been vesting, as now, when the pastor, writing out a Mass card for a parishioner, had flicked his pen at the floor to get the ink flowing. Father Fabre had called his attention to the ink spots on the chasuble. "S'not ink," he'd said. Asked what it was, he's said, "S'not ink," and that was all he'd say. For a time, after that, Father Fabre wondered if the pastor's pen could contain some new kind of writing fluid—not ink—and thought perhaps the spots would disappear. The spots, the *s'not ink* spots, were still there. But a recent incident seemed to explain the pastor's odd denials. "Not a ball point, is it?" he'd said to

Father Fabre who was about to fill his fountain pen from the big bottle in the office. "No, Father," said Father Fabre, presenting his pen for inspection. "Takes ink," said the pastor. "*Yes*, Father." The pastor pointed to the big bottle from which Father Fabre customarily filled his pen, and said, "Why don't you try that?" "Say, that's an idea," said Father Fabre, going the pastor one better. "Better go and flush your pen with water first," said the pastor. And the funny part was that Father Fabre had gone and flushed his pen, before filling it from the big bottle that time. "I think you'll like *that*," said the pastor. *That* was *Quink*. The dormouse had the casuist's gift, and more.

He escaped much of man's fate. Instead of arguing his way out of a jam, or confessing himself in error, the pastor simply denied everything. It was simple—as simple as when he, as priest, changed the bread and wine into the body and blood of Christ. But he had no power from his priesthood to deny the undeniable, for instance that he'd spoiled a good chasuble. When he said "S'not ink," nothing was changed. He could really slow you up, though, if you were inclined to disagree with him and to be rational about it.

When the pastor entered the sacristy before the nine-thirty, Father Fabre was ready for him. "Father," he said, "I can't give this pledge in conscience—not as it's given in some parishes. I can't ask the people to rise as a body and raise their right hands, to repeat after me words which many of them either don't understand the full meaning of, or don't mean to abide by. I don't see anything *wrong* with giving it to those who mean to keep it." He'd wrangled against the pledge in the seminary. If it was "not an oath," as some maintained, wasn't it administered by a priest in church, and didn't it cheapen the clergy to participate in such a ceremony, and one which many merely paid lip service to? Didn't the chancery use the word "invite" and wasn't "demand" the word for the way the thing was rammed through in some parishes? Couldn't outsiders, with some justice, call the whole procedure totalitarian? What *did* Rome think of it? Wasn't it a concession to the rather *different* tone in America, a pacifier?

But the pastor had gone, saying, "Just so you give it."

Father Fabre got behind his servers and started them moving toward the altar. He saw the pastor in front of a battery of vigil lights, picking up the burned matches. Parishioners who had used them would be surprised to know that the pastor blew out all the lights after the last Mass. "Fire hazard," he'd said, caught in the act.

* * *

Before the eleven o'clock, after resting a few minutes between Masses in his room, he went to the bathroom and called down the laundry chute to Miss Burke in the kitchen. "Don't set a place for me. I'm invited out for dinner." He stood ready at the chute to cut her off but heard only a sigh and something about the pastor having said the same thing. He hadn't expected to get away with it so easily. They were having another critical period, and it was necessary, as before, to stand up to her. "I hope I let you know soon enough," he said. She should be happy, with them both gone. She wouldn't have to cook at all. And he was doing her the honor of pretending that she planned their meals ahead.

"Father!"

"Yes, Miss Burke."

"Is it Mrs. Mathers' you're going to?"

He delayed his reply in the hope that she'd see the impertinence of the question, and when this should have been accomplished, he said, "I hope I let you know in time."

He heard the little door slam at the other end of the chute. Then, as always in time of stress, she was speaking intimately to friendly spirits who, of course, weren't there, and then wailing like the wind. "Sure she was puttin' it around she'd have him over! But we none of us"—by which Father Fabre assumed she meant the Altar and Rosary Society—"thought he'd go *there*! Oh, Lord!"

He'd lost the first fall to the pastor, but he'd thrown Miss Burke.

Going downstairs, he heard the coin machines start up in the pastor's room, the tambourines of the separator, the castanets of the counter. The pastor was getting an early start on the day's collections. He wore a green visor in his room and worked under fluorescent tubes. Sometimes he worked a night shift. It was like a war plant, his room, except that no help was wanted. The pastor lived to himself, in a half-light.

In the hallway downstairs, John, the janitor, sitting in the umbrella chair, was having coffee. The chair had a looking-glass back, and when John turned his head he appeared to have two faces.

"Thought you had the day off," said Father Fabre.

"Always plenty to do around here, Father."

"I suppose." They knew each other well enough now for John not to get off that old one about wanting to spend the day with his family.

"She's really rarin' in there," John said. "I had to come out here." He glanced down at the floor, at the cup of muddy water cooling there, and then fearfully in the direction of the kitchen. This did not impress Father Fabre, however, who believed that the janitor and the housekeeper lived in peace. "Not her responsibility," John said.

Father Fabre, knowing he was being tempted, would not discuss the housekeeper with the janitor. Curates came and went, and even pastors, but the janitor, a subtle Slav, stayed on at Trinity.

"I told her it was none of her business."

"*What* isn't?"

"If you want to go there, that's your business," John said. "I had to come out here." John reached down for his cup, without looking, because his hand knew right where it was. "I don't blame you for being sore at her, Father." ("I'm not," Father Fabre murmured, but John, drinking, smiled into his cup.) "I told her it's your business what you do. 'He's old enough,' I said."

"What's she got against Mrs. Mathers?" Father Fabre asked, wondering if Mrs. Mathers was any match for the housekeeper. A natural leader vs. a mental case. It might be close if the Altar and Rosary Society took sides. But the chances were that Miss Burke would soon be fighting on another front. Impossible for her to wage as many wars as she declared.

"Hell, you know how these old maids are, Father," John was saying. "Just needs a man. *You* can understand that."

Father Fabre, calling it a draw with John, turned away and left.

The other guests at Mrs. Mathers' didn't act like Catholics. Mr. Pint, a small man in his sixties, was surprisingly unfriendly, and his daughter, though rather the opposite, went at Father Fabre the wrong way. It might have been the absence of excess respect in her manner that he found unsettling. But Mrs. Mathers, a large, motherly but childless widow with puffy elbows, had baked a cake, and was easy to take.

They were all on the back porch of her second-floor flat, watching Mr. Pint make ice cream.

"Let me taste it, Dad," Velma said.

"I can't be standin' here all day with this cream gettin' soft on me," Mr. Pint said.

Velma pouted. She had on a purple dress which reminded Father Fabre of the purple veils they'd had on the statues in church during Passiontide. Otherwise there was nothing lenten about Velma, he thought.

"If you taste it now," he said, "it'll just take that much longer to harden."

Mr. Pint, who might have agreed with that, said nothing. He dropped a handful of rock salt into the freezer, a wood-and-iron affair that must have been as old as he was, and sank again to his knees. He resumed cranking.

Father Fabre smiled at Mrs. Mathers. Parishioners expected a priest to be nice and jolly, and that was how he meant to be at Mrs. Mathers'. With Mr. Pint setting the tone, it might not be easy. Father Fabre hadn't expected to be the second most important person there.

The cake, he believed, had not been baked for him.

"Your good suit," said Mrs. Mathers. She snatched a *Better Homes and Gardens* from a pile of such magazines and slid it under Mr. Pint's knees.

"Sir Walter Reilly," said Velma, looking at Father Fabre to see if he followed her.

He nodded, doubting her intelligence, wondering if she was bright enough to be a nurse. Mrs. Mathers was a registered nurse.

"Aw, come on," Velma said. "Let me taste it, Dad."

Mr. Pint churned up a chunk of ice and batted it down with the heel of his hand. "By Dad!" he breathed, a little god invoking himself.

Mrs. Mathers wisely retired to the kitchen. Velma, after a moment, ingloriously followed.

Father Fabre gazed over the porch railing. With all the apartment buildings backed up together, it was like a crowded harbor, but with no sign of life—a port of plague. Miss Burke, he remembered, had warned him not to go. John, however, had said go. Mr. Pint's shirt had broken out in patches of deeper blue, and his elastic suspenders, of soft canary hue, were stained a little. Pity moved Father Fabre to offer the helping hand, prudence stayed it, then pity rose again. "Let me take it awhile," he said quietly.

But Mr. Pint, out to deny his size and years,

needed no help, or lost in his exertions, had not heard.

Father Fabre went inside where he found the women, by contrast, laughing and gay. Velma left off tossing the salad, and Mrs. Mathers' stirring spoon hung expectantly in mid-air. "I'm afraid I wasn't much help out there," he said.

"That's just Dad's way," Mrs. Mathers said. "Come in here a minute, Father, if you want to see something nice."

Mrs. Mathers led him into a little room off the kitchen. She wanted him to see her new day bed. He felt the springs as she had and praised the bed in her terms. He meant it when he said he wished he had one, and sat down on it. Mrs. Mathers left the room, and returned a moment later whispering that she believed in flushing the toilet before she made coffee. That was the quickest way to bring fresh water into the house. Father Fabre, rising from the day bed, regretted that he wouldn't be able to pass this household hint on to Miss Burke.

Then, leaving the room, they met Mr. Pint, all salt and sweat, coming in from the back porch. He came among them as one from years at sea, scornful of soft living, suspicious of the women-folk and young stay-at-home males.

The women followed Mr. Pint, and Father Fabre followed the women, into the dining room.

"You're a sight," said Velma.

"Your good blue shirt," said Mrs. Mathers. She went down the hall after Mr. Pint.

"We're going to eat in a minute," Velma said to Father Fabre. "You want to wash or anything?"

"No, thanks," he said. "I never wash."

He had tried to be funny, but Velma seemed ready to believe him.

Mrs. Mathers, looking upset, entered the dining room.

"Should I take off her plate?" Velma asked.

"Leave it on in case she does come," Mrs. Mathers said. "Father, you know Grace."

"No, I don't think so."

"Grace Halloran. She's in the Society."

"Of course." Of course he knew Grace, a maiden lady. He saw her almost daily, a shadow moving around the sanctuary, dusting the altar rail and filling vases with flowers—paid for by herself, the pastor said. Her brother was a big builder of highways. She wasn't the kind to use her means and position, however, to fraternize with the clergy. "Maybe she's just late," he said, rather hoping she wouldn't make it. The present company was difficult enought to assimilate.

Mr. Pint appeared among them again, now wearing a white shirt. Had he brought an extra? Or had Mrs. Mathers given him one which had belonged to her late husband? Father Fabre decided it would be unwise to ask.

They sat down to eat. It was like dining in a convent, with Velma in the role of the nun assigned to him, plying him with food. "Pickles?" He took one and passed the dish to Mr. Pint.

"He can't eat 'em," Velma said.

"That's too bad," said Father Fabre.

Mrs. Mathers, brooding, said: "I can't understand Grace, though heaven knows she can be difficult sometimes."

"If she'd only come," said Velma.

"Yes," said Father Fabre.

"Vel had to work last Sunday and didn't get a chance to meet her," said Mrs. Mathers.

"That's too bad," said Father Fabre.

"Grace was my best friend," Mrs. Mathers said. "In the Society, I mean."

Father Fabre frowned. *Was*?

"I was dying to meet her," said Velma, looking at Father Fabre.

"Very nice person," he said.

"I just can't understand it," declared Mrs. Mathers, without conviction. Then: "It's no surprise to me! You soon find out who your friends are!"

Father Fabre applied his fingers to the fried chicken. "Well," he said. "She doesn't know what she's missing." Grace's plate, however, seemed to reject the statement. "Did she know I was coming?"

"Oh, indeed, she did, Father! That's what makes me so blamed mad!"

Velma went to answer the telephone. "Yoo-hoo! It's for you-hoo!" she called.

"She means you," Mrs. Mathers said to Father Fabre, who wondered how she could have known.

He went to the bedroom, where Mrs. Mathers, never knowing when she'd be called for special duty, had her telephone. When he said "Hello" there was a click and then nothing. "Funny," he said, returning to the table. "Nobody there."

"Vel," Mrs. Mathers asked, "was *that* Grace?"

"She didn't say, Mildred. Wouldn't she say who she was if she was Grace?"

"It was Grace," said Mrs. Mathers quietly. She looked unwell.

There was a rattle of silverware. "Eat your dinner, Mildred," said Mr. Pint, and she did.

After dinner, they retired to the living room. Soon, with Mrs. Mathers and Mr. Pint yawning on the sofa, Velma said, "I met some Catholic priests that were married, once." She had taken the chair near Father Fabre's. They were using the same ash tray.

"Were they Greek or Russian?"

She seemed to think he was joking. "They were with their wives, two of them—I mean they were two couples—but they said the ones that weren't married could have dates with girls if they wanted to."

He nodded. "It's only been observed among us since the eleventh century—celibacy." Velma looked doubtful. "It may be overrated," he added, smiling.

"I never tried it," Velma said.

"Yes, well. . .in some parts of the world, even now, there are married Catholic priests."

"That's what these were," Velma said.

"Maybe they were *Old* Catholics," he said.

"No, they weren't, not at all."

He looked across the room at the couple on the sofa. Mr. Pint appeared to be asleep, but Mrs. Mathers was trying to fight it with a *Good Housekeeping*. "That's a sect," he said, getting back to Velma. "They go by that name. Old Catholics."

"I wouldn't say they were that," she said.

He was ready to drop it.

"I met them in Chicago," she said.

"I understand Old Catholics are strong there," he said. "Comparatively."

There was a lull during which Velma loaded her cigarette case and Father Fabre surveyed the room—the bookcase with no books in it, only plants and bric-a-brac, and the overstuffed furniture rising like bread beneath the slipcovers, which rivaled nature in the tropics for color and variety of growing things, and the upright piano with the mandolin and two photographs on top: one would be the late Mr. Mathers and somewhere in the other, a group picture of graduating nurses, would be the girl he had married, now stout, being now what she had always been becoming. Mrs. Mathers was openly napping now. The room was filled with breathing, hers and Mr. Pint's in unison, and the sun fell upon them all and upon the trembling ferns.

"Mildred says you can't have dates."

Father Fabre looked Velma right in the eye. "That's right." He'd drifted long enough. He'd left the conversation up to her from the beginning, and where had it got him? "I take it you're not a Catholic."

"Oh, no," she said, "but I see all your movies."

"I beg your pardon."

"I liked *The Miracle of the Bells* the best. But they're all swell."

He felt himself drifting again.

"I enjoyed reading *The Cardinal*," she said.

So had he. He wondered if a start could be made there.

Mrs. Mathers, whom he'd thought to be asleep, said "Why don't you tell Father what you told me, Vel?"

"Mildred!" cried Velma.

Father Fabre blushed, thinking Velma must have remarked favorably on his appearance.

"About the church of your choice," said Mrs. Mathers.

"Oh, that. I told Mildred *The Miracle of the Bells* made me want to be a Catholic."

Mr. Pint came to and mumbled something.

Father Fabre decided to face up to him. "Do you like to go to the movies, Mr. Pint?"

"No, sir." Mr. Pint was not looking Father Fabre in the eye, but it was as though he didn't think it necessary—yet.

"Why, Dad," Mrs. Mathers said, "you took me last Sunday night."

"Not to those kind, I didn't. Why'nt you let me finish? By Dad, I ain't so old I can't remember what I did a week back."

"Who said anybody was old?" Velma asked.

"Stop showin' off," Mr. Pint said. "I heard who said it."

Mrs. Mathers clucked sadly, too wise to defend herself.

Mr. Pint blinked at her. "You made me go," he said.

Mrs. Mathers saw her chance. "Ho, ho," she laughed. "I'd just like to see anybody *make* you do anything!"

"You can say that again! Tell him about your office, Dad," Velma said, but Mr. Pint would not.

From the women, however, Father Fabre learned that Mr. Pint had asked "them"—his employers, presumably—to build him an office of glass so that he could sit in it, out of the dirt and noise, and keep an eye on the men who worked under him.

"Why shouldn't they do it," said Mrs. Mathers, "when he saves them all the money he does?"

Father Fabre, about to address Mr. Pint directly, rephrased his question. "He has men under him? I mean—many?"

"Five," said Mrs. Mathers. "Before he came, they had six. He gets more out of five men than they did out of six."

"Two he brought with him," Velma said. "They've been with Dad for years."

Father Fabre nodded. Mr. Pint, with his entourage, was like a big-time football coach, but what was Mr. Pint's work?

Velma, who had switched on the radio, cried, "Lee!"

Father Fabre watched the women closely. Evidently "Lee" was the announcer and not some entertainer to follow on the program. His sponsor, a used car dealer, whose name and address he gave, dispensed with commercial announcements on Sunday, he said, and presented music suited to the day. They sat quietly listening to *How Are Things in Glocca Morra*? Then to *The Rosary,* one of Mrs. Mathers' favorite pieces, she said. Then to *Cryin' in the*

Chapel. Father Fabre wanted to go home.

Lee came on again with the business about no commercials and also threw in the correct time. (Mr. Pint pulled out his watch.) Lee warned motorists to be careful on the highways.

"Don't judge by this. You should hear him on weekdays," Velma said. "Does he ever kid the sponsors!"

"He's a good disc jockey or he wouldn't be on the air," Mrs. Mathers said tartly. "But he's no Arthur Godfrey." It sounded to Father Fabre as though she'd been over this ground with Velma before. "Do you ever get Arthur, Father?"

"Can't say that I do, Mrs. Mathers."

"He might give you some ideas for your sermons."

"My radio isn't working."

"I'll take Lee," Velma said. She rose and went down the hall to the bathroom.

Mrs. Mathers whispered, "Father, did I tell you she wanted to call in for them to play a song for you? *Our Lady of Fatima* or something. She wanted it to come over the air while you were here. A surprise."

"No," he said. "You didn't tell me about that."

"I told her not to do it. I said maybe you wouldn't want it."

"No, I wouldn't." He was grateful to Mrs. Mathers.

Showing a little interest, Mr. Pint inquired uneasily: "What do you think of this disc jockey business?" He got up and turned off the radio.

"I'm afraid I don't know much about it," Father Fabre said, surprised to find himself engaged in conversation with Mr. Pint.

"Sounds kind of fishy to me," said Mr. Pint, sitting down again. He had opened up some, not much, but some. "You know it's just playing phonograph records?"

"Yes," said Father Fabre and then wondered if he'd said the right thing. Mr. Pint might have wanted to tell him about it. Fearing a lull, he plunged. "Certainly was good ice cream."

"Glad you liked it."

After the long winter, gentle spring, the sap running.... "That's a good idea of yours when you make ice cream—bringing an extra shirt, I mean."

There was a bad silence, the worst of the afternoon, crippling every tongue. Even Velma, back with them, was quiet. Mr. Pint was positively stony. Finally, as if seeing no other way, Mrs. Mathers explained:

"Mr. Pint lives here, Father."

"He does?"

"Yes, Father."

"I guess I didn't know."

"I guess I didn't tell you."

"No reason why you should've," he said

quickly. "You do have quite a bit of room here." He seemed to be perspiring. "Certainly do get the sun." He never would have thought it. Was there a chance that Mr. Pint, who acted so strangely, was not her lover? He took a good look at Mr. Pint. Was there a chance that he was? In either case, Mrs. Mathers had planned well. Father Fabre, taking out his handkerchief, blew his nose politely and dabbed at his cold, damp neck. He was in very good health and perspired freely. The fat flowery arms of the overstuffed chair held him fast while the hidden mouth devoured him. The trembling ferns frankly desired him. He just never would have thought it.

"You should see my little room at the Y," Velma said. "So dark." She was looking at Father Fabre, but he could think of nothing to say.

Mrs. Mathers sighed, "Vel, you *could* stay here, you know. She could too." Mrs. Mathers appealed to Father Fabre. "The day bed is always ready."

"Oh, well," said Velma.

"So I had this extra bedroom," Mrs. Mathers said, as if coming to the end of a long explanation, "and I thought I might as well have the income from it—what's your opinion, Father?"

"Swell," he said. In the future he ought to listen to Miss Burke and stay away from John, with his rotten talk against her. A very sound person, Miss Burke, voices, visions and all. He ought to develop a retiring nature, too, stick close to the pastor, maybe try to get a job in his war plant. "I hate to rush off," he said, rising.

"Don't tell me it's time for devotions," said Mrs. Mathers.

They went down the street together. "You know, Father," said Mrs. Mathers. "I almost asked them to come along with us."

"You did?" Mrs. Mathers was hard to figure. He'd heard that hospital life made iconoclasts.

"What'd you think of Vel?"

"Who? Oh, fine." He didn't know what he thought of Vel. "What does she do?"

"She's with the telephone company, Father. She thinks she's in line for a supervisor's, but I don't know. The seniority system is the one big thing in her favor. Of course, it wouldn't come right away."

"I suppose not," Father Fabre said. "She seems quite young for that."

"Yes, and they're pretty careful about those jobs."

"What I understand." He was in line for a pastor's himself. They were pretty careful about those jobs too. "What does Mr. Pint do?"

"Didn't I tell you?"

"No," he said bleakly.

Mr. Pint was an engineer. "But he never touches a wrench. He's like an executive."

"Where?"

"At the hospital, Father."

"At City?"

"At Mercy, Father."

Oh God, he thought, the nuns were going to be in on it too. They walked the next block in silence.

"Who plays the mandolin?" he asked.

"He does."

They walked another block in silence. "I don't want to get TV," she said plaintively. She brightened at the sight of a squirrel.

"Don't care for TV?"

"No, it's not that. I just don't know how long I'll keep my apartment."

Was Mrs. Mathers saying that she'd get out of town, or only that she'd move to another parish? If so, she was a little late. By feasting at their board, he had blessed the union, if any, in the eyes of the parish. What a deal! It was too late for him to condemn the enamored couple, one of whom was out of his jurisdiction anyway (in parting he had shaken Mr. Pint's hand). It was a bad situation, bad in itself and bad because it involved him. Better, though, that they live in sin than marry in haste. That was something, however, that it would take theologians (contemplating the dangers of mixed marriage, the evil of divorce) to see. He knew what the parishioners would think of that.

And the pastor...

At the church, at the moment of parting, he said, "You're going to be early for devotions." That was all. To thank her, as he wanted to, for the good dinner would be, in a way, to thank her for compromising him with parish and pastor. It was quite enough that he say nothing to hurt her, and go.

"I've got some things to do around the side altars," Mrs. Mathers said.

He nodded, backing away.

"You suppose Grace'll be inside?" she called after him, just as if all were now well between her and her best friend in the Society.

He had his back to her and kept going, plowed on, nodding though, vigorously nodding like one of the famous yes-horses of Odense. For a moment he entertained the idea that Mrs. Mathers was a mental case, which would explain everything, but it wouldn't do. Mrs. Mathers remained a mystery to him.

In the rectory, he started up the front stairs for his room. Then he went back down, led by sounds to the converts' parlor. There he found a congregation of middle-aged women dressed mostly in navy blues and blacks, unmistakably Altar and Rosary, almost a full consistory, and swarming.

"Could I be of any service to you ladies?"

The swarming let up. "Miss Burke said we should wait in here," someone said.

He hadn't seen who had spoken. "For me?" he said, looking them over. He saw Grace sorrowing in their midst.

"No, Father," said someone else, also hidden from him. "We're here to see the pastor."

"Oh," he said.

"*He* went out on a sick call," said someone else.

"Oh," he said, and escaped.

One minute later he was settling down in the garage, on the bottom rung of a folding ladder, the best seat he could find. He picked up a wrench, got grease on his fingers, and remembered that Mr. Pint never touched a wrench. He wondered where he'd gone wrong, if there was anything he might have done, or might yet do. There was nothing. He attributed his trouble to his belief, probably mistaken, that the chancery had wanted a man at Trinity to compensate for the pastor. Father Fabre had tried to be that man, one who would be accessible to the people. The pastor strenuously avoided people. He was happy with the machines in his room, or on a picnic with himself, topped off perhaps with a visit to the zoo. The assistant was the one to see at Trinity. Naturally there were people who would try to capitalize on his inexperience. The pastor gave him a lot of rope. Some pastors wouldn't let their curates dine out with parishioners—with good reason, it appeared. The pastor was watchful, though, and would rein in the rope on the merest suspicion. Father Fabre was thinking of the young lady of charm and education who had come to him after Mass on Sunday with the idea of starting up a study club at Trinity. He'd told the pastor and the pastor had told him, "It's under study." You might think that would be the end of it. It had been, so far as the young lady was concerned, but that evening at table Father Fabre was asked by the dormouse if he knew about young ladies.

"Know about them?"

"Ummm." The dormouse was feasting on a soda cracker.

"Well, Father. I had them all in a sodality some years ago." (Ordinarily untalkative to the point of being occult, the pastor spoke now as a man compelled, and Father Fabre attended his every word. The seminary professors had harped on the wisdom of pastors, as against the all-consuming ignorance of curates). It seemed that the pastor, being so busy, didn't notice how the young ladies showed up for induction during the few years of the sodality's existence at Trinity, but from the day he did, there had been no more of that. (*What*? Father Fabre wondered but did not interrupt.) The pastor was not narrow-minded, he said, and he granted that a young woman might wear a bit of paint on her wedding day. But when sodalists, dedicated to the Blessed Virgin, the Mother of God, Mary Immaculate, presented themselves at the communion rail in low-necked evening gowns, wearing lipstick, stuff in their eyes, and with their hair up in the permanent wave, why then, Gentlemen—the pastor used that word, causing Father Fabre to blink and then to realize that he was hearing a speech the pastor must have given at a clergy conference—there was something wrong somewhere and that was why he had suppressed the sodality in his parish.

By God, thought Father Fabre, nodding vigorously, the pastor had a point! Here was something to remember if he ever got a church of his own.

It must have touched the pastor to see his point so well taken by his young curate, for he smiled. "You might say the scales dropped from my eyes," he said.

But by then Father Fabre, gazing at the cracker flake on the pastor's black bosom, had begun to wonder what all this had to do with a study club, and must have shown it.

"A study club's just another name for a sodality," the pastor prompted. "See what I mean?"

Father Fabre did not, not unless the pastor

meant that young ladies were apt to belong to either and that, therefore, his curate would do well to steer clear of both. Hear their sins, visit them in sickness and prison, give them the Sacrament. Beyond that, there wasn't much to be done for or about them. In time they would get old and useful. The pastor, for his part, had put them away in the cellar part of his mind to ripen like cheese. But the good ladies of the Altar and Rosary were something else again. Nuns could not have kept the church cleaner, and the good ladies, unlike nuns, didn't labor under the illusion that they were somehow priests, only different, and so weren't always trying to vault the communion rail to the altar.

"You want to be one of these 'youth priests,' Father?"

"I haven't thought much about it."

"Good."

But, as the pastor must have noticed, Father Fabre had wanted to get some "activities" going at Trinity, believing that his apostolate lay in the world, with the people, as the pastor's obviously didn't. Well, he had failed. But he wasn't sorry. Wasn't there enough to do at Trinity, just doing the regular chores? For the poor, the sick and dying, yes, anything. But non-essentials he'd drop, including dining out with parishioners, and major decisions he'd cheerfully hand over to the pastor. (He still thought the man who rented owls to rid you of pigeons might have something, for that was nature's way, no cruel machines or powders. But he'd stop agitating for the owls, for that was another problem for the pastor to solve, or, probably, not to solve.) Of course the parish was indifferently run, but wasn't it a mistake to keep trying to take up *all* the slack? He'd had himself under observation, of late. It seemed to him his outlook was changing, not from a diminution of zeal, not from loss of vision, but from growing older and wiser. At least he hoped so. He was beginning to believe he wasn't the man to compensate for the pastor—not that he'd ask for a transfer. The bishop was a gentle administrator but always seemed to find a place in one of the salt mines for a young man seeking a change. Father Fabre's predecessor in the curate's job at Trinity had been anti-social, which some of the gadabout clergy said could be a grievous fault in a parish priest, but he hadn't asked for a change—it had come to him—and now he was back in the seminary, as a professor with little pocket money, it was true, but enjoying food and handball again. That afternoon, sitting in the garage, Father Fabre envied him.

The pastor handed a wicker basket to Father Fabre, and himself carried a thermos bottle. He showed no surprise at finding his curate waiting for him in the garage and asked no questions. Father Fabre, the moment he saw the basket and bottle, understood that the pastor was returning from a picnic, and that Miss Burke, telling the ladies he'd gone on a sick call, thought it part of her job to create a good impression whenever possible, part of being loyal, the prime requisite. Who but the pastor would have her for a housekeeper?

They walked to the back door at the pastor's pace.

"Some coffee in here for you," the pastor said, jiggling the thermos bottle.

"Thanks," said Father Fabre, but he'd not be having any of that.

"One of the bears died at Como," the pastor said. "One of the babies."

"That's too bad," said Father Fabre. He pushed in the door for the pastor, then stood aside. "Some women to see you in the converts' parlor," he said, as the pastor passed in front of him.

The pastor nodded. Women in the converts' parlor; he would see them.

"I don't know," Father Fabre said. "It may concern me—indirectly." Then, staring down at the kitchen linoleum, he began an account of his afternoon at Mrs. Mathers'. At the worst part—his chagrin on learning of the set-up there—the pastor interrupted. He filled an unwashed cup from the sink with the fluid from the thermos bottle, gave it to Father Fabre to drink, and watched to see that he did. Father Fabre drank Miss Burke's foul coffee to the dregs and chewed up a few grounds. When he started up his account again, the pastor interrupted.

"That's enough," he said.

Father Fabre, for a moment, thought he was in for it. But when he looked into the pastor's eyes, there was nothing in them for him to fear, nor was there fear, nor even fear of fear, bravado. The pastor's eyes were blue, blank and blue.

Father Fabre followed the pastor at a little distance, out of the kitchen, down the hallway. "Will you need me?" he said.

With an almost imperceptible shake of his head, the pastor walked into the converts' parlor, leaving the door ajar as always when dealing with women.

Father Fabre stayed to listen, out of sight of those inside. He soon realized that it had been a mistake to omit all mention of Velma in his account, as he had, thinking her presence at Mrs. Mathers' incidental, her youth likely to sidetrack the pastor, to arouse memories of so-called study clubs and suppressed sodalists. Why, if the pastor was to hear the details, didn't they tell him that Grace had been invited to dinner? Then there would have been five of them. The pastor was sure to get the wrong impression. To hear the ladies tell it, Mr. Pint and Father Fabre were as bad as sailors on leave, kindred evil spirits double-dating a couple of dazzled working girls. The ladies weren't being fair to Father Fabre or, he felt, even to Mr. Pint. He wondered at the pastor's silence. When all was said and done, there was little solidarity among priests—a nest of tables scratching each other.

In the next room, it was the old, old story, right from Scripture, the multitude crying, "Father, this woman was taken in adultery. The law commandeth us to stone such a one. What sayest thou?" The old story with the difference that the pastor had nothing to say. Why didn't he say: She that is without sin among you, let her first cast a stone at her! But there was one close by who could and would speak, who knew what it was to have the mob against him, and who was not afraid. With chapter and verse he'd atomize 'em. *This day thou shouldst be pastor*. Yes, it did look that way, but he'd wait a bit, to give the pastor a chance to redeem himself. He imagined how it would be if he hit them with that text. They, hearing him, would go out one by one, even the pastor, from that day forward his disciple. And he alone would remain, and the woman. And he, lifting up himself, would say, Woman, where are they that accused thee? Hath no one condemned thee? Who would say, No one, master. Neither will I condemn thee. Go, and sin no more.

"Think he can handle it?"

Whirling, Father Fabre beheld his tempter. "Be gone, John," he said, and watched the janitor slink away.

Father Fabre, after that, endeavored to think well of the pastor, to discover the meaning in his silence. Was this forbearance? It seemed more like paralysis. The bomb was there to be used, but the pastor couldn't or wouldn't use it. He'd have to do something, though. The ladies, calmed at first by his silence, sounded restless. Soon they might regard his silence not as response to a grave problem but as refusal to hold council with them.

"We don't feel it's any of our business to know *what* you intend to do, Father, but we would like some assurance that something will be done. Is that asking too much?"

The pastor said nothing.

"We thought you'd know what to do, Father," said another. "What would be best for all concerned, Father. Gosh, I don't know what to think!"

The pastor cleared his throat, touched, possibly, by the last speaker's humility, but he said nothing.

"I wonder if we've made ourselves clear," said the one who had spoken before the last one. She wasn't speaking to the pastor but to the multitude. "Maybe that's what comes from trying to describe everything in the best possible light." (Father Fabre remembered the raw deal they'd given him.) "Not *all* of us, I'm afraid, believe that man's there against Mildred's will."

"*S'not so.*"

Father Fabre gasped. Oh, no! Not that! But yes, the pastor had spoken.

"Father, do you mean to say we're lying?"

"*No.*"

Father Fabre shook his head. In all arguments with the pastor there was a place like the Sargasso Sea, and the ladies had reached it. It was authority that counted then, as Father Fabre knew, who had always lacked it. The ladies hadn't taken a vow of obedience, though, and they might not take "S'not so" for an answer. They might very well go to the chancery. At the prospect of that, of the fine slandering he'd get there, and realizing only then that he and the pastor were in the same boat, Father Fabre began to consider the position as defined by "S'not so" and "No." The pastor was saying (a) that the situation, as reported by the ladies, was not so, and (b) that the ladies were not lying. He seemed to be contradicting himself, as was frequently the case in disputations with his curate. This was no intramural spat, however. The pastor would have to make sense for a change, to come out on top. *Could* the dormouse be right? And the ladies wrong in what they thought? What if what they thought was just not so? *Honi soit qui mal y pense*?

One said, "I just can't understand Mildred," but Father Fabre thought he could, now. At no time had Mrs. Mathers sounded guilty, and that—her seeming innocence—was what had thrown everything out of kilter. When she said Mr. Pint lived with her, when she said she was thinking of giving up her apartment, she had sounded not guilty but regretful, regretful and flustered, as though she knew that her friends and even her clergy were about to desert her. Mrs. Mathers was a veteran nurse, the human body was her work bench, sex probably a matter of technical concern, as with elderly plumbers who distinguish between the male and female connections. It was quite possible that Mrs. Mathers had thought nothing of letting a room to a member of the opposite sex. She could not have known that what was only an economy measure for her would appear to others as something very different—and so, in fact, it had become for her, in time. Mrs. Mathers and Mr. Pint were best described as victims of their love for each other. It was true love, of that Father Fabre was now certain. He had only to recollect it. If it were the other kind, Mrs. Mathers never would have invited him over—and Grace—to meet Mr. Pint. Mr. Pint, non-Catholic and priest-shy, had never really believed that Mrs. Mathers' friends would understand, and when Grace defaulted, he had become sullen, ready to take on anybody, even a priest, which showed the quality of his regard for Mrs. Mathers, that he meant to marry her willy nilly, in or out of the Church. There must be no delay. All Mrs. Mathers needed now, all she'd ever needed, was a little time—and help. If she could get Mr. Pint to take instructions, they could have a church wedding. Velma, already Catholic in spirit, could be bridesmaid. That was it. The ladies had done their worst—Father Fabre's part in the affair was criminally exaggerated—but the pastor, the angelic dormouse, had not failed to sniff out the benign object of Mrs. Mathers' grand plan. Or what would have been its object. The ladies could easily spoil everything.

One of the ladies got sarcastic. "Would it be too much to ask, then, just what do you mean?"

The pastor said nothing.

Then the one who earlier had succeeded in getting him to clear his throat said, "Father, it's not always easy for us to understand everything you say. Now, Father, I always get a lot out of your sermons—why, some I've heard on television aren't half as good—but I don't kid myself that I can understand *every* word you say. Still waters run deep, I guess, and I haven't got the education

I should have. So, Father, would you please tell us what you mean, in words we can all understand?"

It would have surprised Father Fabre if, after all that, the pastor had said nothing.

"*S'not so*," he said.

Father Fabre had to leave then, for devotions.

In the sacristy, he slipped into his cassock, eased the zipper past the spot where it stuck, pawed the hangers for his surplice, found it on the floor. The altar boys had come, but he wasn't in the mood for them, for the deceptive small talk that he seemed to do so well, from ballplayers to St. John Bosco in one leap, using the Socratic method to get them to do their own thinking and then breaking off the conversation when he'd brought out the best in them. It wasn't necessary with the two on hand—twins who were going to be priests anyway, according to them at the age of ten. They had fired the censer too soon, and it would be petering out after the rosary, when it would be needed for benediction. He stood at the door of the sacristy and gazed out into the almost empty church. It was the nice weather that kept people away from devotions, it was said, and it was the bad weather that kept them away in the wintertime. He saw Mrs. Mathers kneeling alone in prayer. The pastor had done well for her, everything considered, but not well enough, Father Fabre feared. He feared a scandal. Great schisms from little squabbles grew....

And great affirmations! He'd expected the pastor to dismiss the ladies in time for devotions, but he hadn't expected them to come, not in such numbers, and he took it as a sign from heaven when they didn't kneel apart from Mrs. Mathers, the woman taken in adultery, or thereabouts; a sign that the pastor had triumphed, as truth must always triumph over error, sooner or later, always: that was heaven's promise to pastors. Life was a dark business for everyone in it, but the way for pastors was ever lit by flares of special grace. Father Fabre, knowing full well that he, in spirit, had been no better than the ladies, thanked God for the little patience he'd had, and asked forgiveness for thinking ill of the pastor, for coveting his authority. He who would have been proud to hurl the ready answer at Mrs. Mathers' persecutors, to stone them back, to lose the ninety-nine sheep and save not the one whose innocence he would have violated publicly then as he had in his heart, in his heart humbled himself with thoughts of his unworthiness, marveled at the great good lesson he'd learned that day from the pastor, that Solomon. But the pastor, he knew, was zealous in matters affecting the common weal, champion of decency in his demesne, and might have a word or two for his curate at the table that evening, and for Mrs. Mathers there would certainly be a just poke or two from the blunt sword of his mercy.

Father Fabre, trailing the boys out of the sacristy, gazed upon the peaceful flock, and then beyond, in a dim, dell-like recess of the nave used for baptism, he saw the shepherd carrying a stick and then he heard him opening a few windows.

A SICK CALL
by Morley Callaghan

I

SOMETIMES Father Macdowell mumbled out loud and took a deep wheezy breath as he walked up and down the room and read his office. He was a huge old priest, white-headed except for a shiny baby-pink bald spot on the top of his head, and he was a bit deaf in one ear. His florid face had many fine red interlacing vein lines. For hours he had been hearing confessions and he was tired, for he always had to hear more confessions than any other priest at the cathedral; young girls who were in trouble, and wild but at times repentant young men, always wanted to tell their confessions to Father Macdowell, because nothing seemed to shock or excite him, or make him really angry, and he was even tender with those who thought they were most guilty.

While he was mumbling and reading and trying to keep his glasses on his nose, the house girl knocked on the door and said, "There's a young lady here to see you, Father. I think it's about a sick call."

"Did she ask for me especially?" he said in a deep but slightly cracked voice.

"Indeed she did, Father. She wanted Father Macdowell and nobody else."

So he went out to the waiting room, where a girl about thirty years of age, with fine brown eyes, fine cheek bones, and rather square shoulders, was sitting daubing her eyes with a handkerchief. She was wearing a dark coat with a gray wolf collar. "Good evening, Father," she said. "My sister is sick. I wanted you to come and see her. We think she's dying."

"Be easy, child; what's the matter with her? Speak louder. I can hardly hear you."

"My sister's had pneumonia. The doctor's coming back to see her in an hour. I wanted you to anoint her, Father."

"I see, I see. But she's not lost yet. I'll not give her extreme unction now. That may not be necessary. I'll go with you and hear her confession."

"Father, I ought to let you know, maybe. Her husband won't want to let you see her. He's not a Catholic, and my sister hasn't been to church in a long time."

"Oh, don't mind that. He'll let me see her," Father Macdowell said, and he left the room to put on his hat and coat.

II

When he returned, the girl explained that her name was Jane Stanhope, and her sister lived only a few blocks away. "We'll walk and you tell me about your sister,'' he said. He put his black hat square on his head, and pieces of white hair stuck out awkwardly at the sides. They went to the avenue together.

The night was mild and clear. Miss Stanhope began to walk slowly, because Father Macdowell's rolling gait didn't get him along the street very quickly. He walked as if his feet hurt him, though he wore a pair of large, soft, specially constructed shapeless shoes. ''Now, my child, you go ahead and tell me about your sister,'' he said, breathing with difficulty, yet giving the impression that nothing could have happened to the sister which would make him feel indignant.

There wasn't much to say, Miss Stanhope replied. Her sister had married John Williams two years ago, and he was a good, hard-working fellow, only he was very bigoted and hated all church people. ''My family wouldn't have anything to do with Elsa after she married him, though I kept going to see her,'' she said. She was talking in a loud voice to Father Macdowell so he could hear her.

''Is she happy with her husband?''

''She's been very happy, Father. I must say that.''

''Where is he now?''

''He was sitting beside her bed. I ran out

because I thought he was going to cry. He said if I brought a priest near the place he'd break the priest's head."

"My goodness. Never mind, though. Does your sister want to see me?"

"She asked me to go and get a priest, but she doesn't want John to know she did it."

III

Turning into a side street, they stopped at the first apartment house, and the old priest followed Miss Stanhope up the stairs. His breath came with great difficulty. "Oh dear, I'm not getting any younger, not one day younger. It's a caution how a man's legs go back on him," he said. As Miss Stanhope rapped on the door, she looked pleadingly at the old priest, trying to ask him not to be offended at anything that might happen, but he was smiling and looking huge in the narrow hallway. He wiped his head with his handkerchief.

The door was opened by a young man in a white shirt with no collar, with a head of thick black wavy hair. At first he looked dazed, then his eyes got bright with excitement when he saw the priest, as though he were glad to see someone he could destroy with pent-up energy. "What do you mean, Jane?" he said. "I told you not to bring a priest around here. My wife doesn't want to see a priest."

"What's that you're saying, young man?"

"No one wants you here."

"Speak up. Don't be afraid. I'm a bit hard of hearing." Father Macdowell smiled rosily. John Williams was confused by the unexpected deafness in the priest, but he stood there, blocking the door with sullen resolution as if waiting for the priest to try to launch a curse at him.

"Speak to him, Father," Miss Stanhope said, but the priest didn't seem to hear her; he was still smiling as he pushed past the young man, saying, "I'll go in and sit down, if you don't mind, son. I'm here on God's errand, but I don't mind saying I'm all out of breath from climbing those stairs."

John was dreadfully uneasy to see he had been brushed aside, and he followed the priest into the apartment and said loudly, "I don't want you here."

Father Macdowell said, "Eh, eh?" Then he smiled sadly. "Don't be angry with me, son," he said. "I'm too old to try and be fierce and threatening." Looking around, he said, "Where's your wife?" and he started to walk along the hall, looking for the bedroom.

John followed him and took hold of his arm. "There's no sense in your wasting your time talking to my wife, do you hear?" he said angrily.

Miss Stanhope called out suddenly, "Don't be rude, John."

"It's he that's being rude. You mind your

business,'' John said.

''For the love of God let me sit down a moment with her, anyway. I'm tired,'' the priest said.

''What do you want to say to her? Say it to me, why don't you?''

IV

Then they both heard someone moan softly in the adjoining room, as if the sick woman had heard them. Father Macdowell, forgetting that the young man had hold of his arm, said, ''I'll go in and see her for a moment, if you don't mind,'' and he began to open the door.

''You're not going to be alone with her, that's all,'' John said, following him into the bedroom.

Lying on the bed was a white-faced, fair girl, whose skin was so delicate that her cheek bones stood out sharply. She was feverish, but her eyes rolled toward the door, and she watched them coming in. Father Macdowell took off his coat, and as he mumbled to himself he looked around the room at the mauve-silk bed and the light wall-paper with the tiny birds in fight. It looked like a little girl's room. ''Good evening, Father,'' Mrs. Williams whispered. She looked scared. She didn't glance at her husband. The notion of dying had made her afraid. She loved her husband and wanted to die loving him, but she was afraid, and she looked up at the priest.

"You're going to get well, child," Father Macdowell said, smiling and patting her hand gently.

John, who was standing stiffly by the door, suddenly moved around the big priest, and he bent down over the bed and took his wife's hand and began to caress her forehead.

"Now, if you don't mind, my son, I'll hear your wife's confession," the priest said.

"No, you won't," John said abruptly. "Her people didn't want her, and they left us together, and they're not going to separate us now. She's satisfied with me." He kept looking down at her face as if he could not bear to turn away.

Father Macdowell nodded his head up and down and sighed. "Poor boy," he said. "God bless you." Then he looked at Mrs. Williams, who had closed her eyes, and he saw a faint tear on her cheek. "Be sensible, my boy," he said. "You'll have to let me hear your wife's confession. Leave us alone awhile."

"I'm going to stay right here," John said, and he sat down on the end of the bed. He was working himself up and staring savagely at the priest. All of a sudden he noticed the tears on his wife's cheeks, and he muttered as though bewildered, "What's the matter, Elsa? What's the matter, darling? Are we bothering you? Just open your eyes and we'll go out of the room and leave you alone till the doctor comes." Then he turned and said to the priest, "I'm not going to leave you here with her, can't you see that? Why don't you go?"

"I could revile you, my son. I could threaten you; but I ask you, for the peace of your wife's soul, leave us alone." Father Macdowell spoke with patient tenderness. He looked very big and solid and immovable as he stood by the bed. "I liked your face as soon as I saw you," he said to John. "You're a good fellow."

John still held his wife's wrist, but he rubbed one hand through his thick hair and said angrily, "You don't get the point, sir. My wife and I were always left alone, and we merely want to be left alone now. Nothing is going to separate us. She's been content with me. I'm sorry, sir; you'll have to speak to her with me here, or you'll have to go."

"No; you'll have to go for a while," the priest said patiently.

V

Then Mrs. Williams moved her head on the pillow and said jerkily, "Pray for me, Father."

So the old priest knelt down by the bed, and with a sweet unruffled expression on his florid face he began to pray. At times his breath came with a whistling noise as though a rumbling were inside him, and at other times he sighed and was full of sorrow. He was praying that young Mrs.

Williams might get better, and while he prayed he knew that her husband was more afraid of losing her to the Church than losing her to death.

All the time Father Macdowell was on his knees, with his heavy prayer book in his two hands, John kept staring at him. John couldn't understand the old priest's patience and tolerance. He wanted to quarrel with him, but he kept on watching the light from overhead shining on the one baby-pink bald spot on the smooth white head, and at last he burst out, "You don't understand, sir! We've been very happy together. Neither you nor her people came near her when she was in good health, so why should you bother her now? I don't want anything to separate us now; neither does she. She came with me. You see you'd be separating us, don't you?" He was trying to talk like a reasonable man who had no prejudices.

Father Macdowell got up clumsily. His knees hurt him, for the floor was hard. He said to Mrs. Williams in quite a loud voice, "Did you really intend to give up everything for this young fellow?" and he bent down close to her so he could hear.

"Yes, Father," she whispered.

"In Heaven's name, child, you couldn't have known what you were doing."

"We loved each other, Father. We've been very happy."

"All right. Supposing you were. What now? What about all eternity, child?"

"Oh, Father, I'm very sick and I'm afraid." She looked up to try to show him how scared she was, and how much she wanted him to give her peace.

He sighed and seemed distressed, and at last he said to John, "Were you married in the church?"

"No, we weren't. Look here, we're talking pretty loud and it upsets her."

"Ah, it's a crime that I'm hard of hearing, I know. Never mind, I'll go." Picking up his coat, he put it over his arm; then he sighed as if he were very tired, and he said, "I wonder if you'd just fetch me a glass of water. I'd thank you for it."

John hesitated, glancing at the tired old priest, who looked so pink and white and almost cherubic in his utter lack of guile.

"What's the matter?" Father Macdowell said.

John was ashamed of himself for appearing so sullen, so he said hastily, "Nothing's the matter. Just a moment. I won't be a moment." He hurried out of the room.

VI

The old priest looked down at the floor and shook his head; and then, sighing and feeling uneasy, he bent over Mrs. Williams, with his good ear down to her, and he said, "I'll just ask you a few questions in a hurry, my child. You answer them quickly and I'll give you absolution." He made the sign of the cross over her and asked if she repented for having strayed from the Church, and if she had often been angry, and whether she had always been faithful, and if she had ever lied or stolen—all so casually and quickly as if it hadn't occurred to him that such a young woman could have serious sins. In the same breath he muttered, "Say a good act of contrition to yourself and that will be all, my dear." He had hardly taken a minute.

When John returned to the room with the glass of water in his hand, he saw the old priest making the sign of the cross. Father Macdowell went on praying without even looking up at John. When he had finished, he turned and said, "Oh, there you are. Thanks for the water. I needed it. Well, my boy, I'm sorry if I worried you."

John hardly said anything. He looked at his wife, who had closed her eyes, and he sat down on the end of the bed. He was too disappointed to speak.

Father Macdowell, who was expecting trouble, said, "Don't be harsh, lad."

"I'm not harsh," he said mildly, looking up at the priest. "But you weren't quite fair. And it's as though she turned away from me at the last moment. I didn't think she needed you."

"God bless you, bless the both of you. She'll get better," Father Macdowell said. But he felt ill at ease as he put on his coat, and he couldn't look directly at John.

VII

Going along the hall, he spoke to Miss Stanhope, who wanted to apologize for her brother-in-law's attitude. "I'm sorry if it was unpleasant for you, Father," she said.

"It wasn't unpleasant," he said. "I was glad to meet John. He's a fine fellow. It's a great pity he isn't a Catholic. I don't know as I played fair with him."

As he went down the stairs, puffing and sighing, he pondered the question of whether he had played fair with the young man. But by the time he reached the street he was rejoicing amiably to think he had so successfully ministered to one who had strayed from the faith and had called out to him at the last moment. Walking along with the rolling motion as if his feet hurt him, he muttered, "Of course they were happy as they were . . . in a worldly way. I wonder if I did come between them?"

He shuffled along, feeling tired, but he couldn't help thinking, "What beauty there was to his staunch love for her!" Then he added quickly, "But it was just a pagan beauty, of course."

As he began to wonder about the nature of this beauty, for some reason he felt inexpressibly sad.

DEATH IN JERUSALEM
by William Trevor

"TILL then," Father Paul said, leaning out of the window of the train for Dublin. "Till Jerusalem, Francis."

"Please God, Paul." As Francis spoke, the train began to move, and his brother waved from the window and he waved back, a modest figure on the platform. Everyone in the town said Francis might have been a priest as well, meaning that Francis's quietness and meditative disposition had an air of the cloister about them. But Francis contented himself with the running of Daly's hardware business, which his mother had run until she was too old for it. "Are we game for the Holy Land next year?" Father Paul had repeatedly asked that July, during his annual visit home. "Will we go together, Francis?" He had brushed aside all Francis's protestations, all attempts to explain that the shop could not be left, that their mother would be confused by the absence of Francis from the house. Rumbustiously Father Paul had pointed out that their sister Kitty was in charge of the household of which Francis and their mother were part, and that Kitty's husband, Myles, could surely be trusted to look after the shop for a single fortnight. For thirty years, ever since he was seven,

Francis had wanted to go to the Holy Land. He had savings that he'd never spent a penny of; you can't take it with you, Father Paul had stated more than once.

On the platform Francis watched until the train could no longer be seen, his thoughts still with his brother. The priest's ruddy countenance smiled again behind cigarette smoke; his bulk remained impressive in the clerical clothes—the collar pinching the flesh of his neck, his black shoes scrupulously polished. There were freckles on the backs of his large, strong hands; he had a fine head of hair, gray and crinkly. In an hour and a half's time the train would creep into Dublin, and he'd take a taxi. He'd spend a night in the Gresham Hotel before catching his plane back to America. In the bar he'd probably fall in with another priest, have a drink or two, maybe play a game of bridge after his meal. That was his brother's way and always had been—an extravagant, easy way of smiles and good humor. It was what had taken him to America in the first place and made him successful there. In order to raise money for the church that he and Father Steigmuller intended to build by 1980, he took parties of the well-to-do from San Francisco to Rome and Florence, to Chartres and Seville and the Holy Land. He was good at raising money—not just for the church but for the boys' home of which he was president, and for the

Hospital of Our Saviour, and for St. Mary's Old People's Home, on the west side of the city. But every July he flew back to Ireland, to the town in County Tipperary where his mother and brother and sister still lived. He stayed in the house above the shop, which he might have inherited himself on the death of his father, which he'd rejected in favor of the religious life. Mrs. Daly was eighty now. In the shop she sat silently behind the counter, in a corner by the chicken wire, wearing black clothes only. In the evenings she sat with Francis in the lace-curtained sitting room while the rest of the family occupied the kitchen. It was for her sake most of all that Father Paul made the journey every summer, considering it his duty.

Walking back to the town from the station, Francis was aware that he was missing his brother. Paul was fourteen years older and in childhood had often taken the place of their father, who had died when Francis was five. His brother had possessed enviable strength and knowledge; he'd been a hero, an example of success. In later life he had become an example of generosity as well: ten years ago he'd taken their mother to Rome, and their sister Kitty and her husband two years later; he'd paid the expenses when their sister Edna had gone to Canada; he'd helped two nephews to make a start in America. Francis, in childhood, hadn't had a healthy freckled face like his brother's, just as in middle age he didn't have a ruddy complexion and a stoutness and an easiness with people. Francis was slight, his sandy hair receding, his face rather pale. His breathing was sometimes labored because of wheeziness in the chest. In the hardware shop he wore a brown cotton coat.

"Hullo, Mr. Daly," a woman said to him on his way from the station. "Father Paul's gone off, has he?"

"Yes, he's gone again."

"I'll pray for his journey so," the woman promised, and Francis thanked her.

A year went by. In San Francisco another wing of the boys' home was completed and another target was reached in Father Paul and Father Steigmuller's fund for the church they planned to have built by 1980. In the town in County Tipperary there were baptisms and burial services and First Communions. Old Loughlin, a farmer from Bansha, died in Flynn's grocery and bar, having gone there to celebrate a good price he'd got for a heifer. Clancy, from behind the counter in Doran's drapery, married Maureen Talbot; Mr. Nolan's plasterer married Miss Driscoll; Johneen Lynch married Seamus from the chips shop, under pressure from her family to do so. A local horse, from the stables on the Limerick road, was said to be an entry for the Fairyhouse

Grand National, but it turned out not to be true.

Every evening of that year Francis sat with his mother in the lace-curtained sitting room above the shop. Every weekday she sat in her corner by the chicken wire, watching while he counted out screws and weighed staples, or advised about yard brushes or tap washers. Occasionally, on a Saturday, he visited the three Christian Brothers who lodged with Mrs. Shea, and afterward he'd tell his mother about how the authority was slipping these days from the nuns and the Christian Brothers, and how Mrs. Shea's elderly maid, Agnes, couldn't see to cook the food anymore. His mother would nod and hardly ever speak. When he told a joke—what young Hogan had said when he'd found a nail in his egg, or how Agnes had put mint sauce into a jug with milk in it—she never laughed, and looked at him in surprise when he laughed himself. But Dr. Grady said it was best to keep her cheered up.

All during that year Francis talked to her about his forthcoming visit to the Holy Land, endeavoring to make her understand that for a fortnight the next spring he would be away from the house and shop. He'd been away before for odd days, but that was when she was younger. He had sometimes visited an aunt in Tralee, but the aunt had died, and he hadn't left the town for three years.

Francis and his mother had always been close.

Before his birth two daughters had died in infancy, and his very survival had struck Mrs. Daly as a gift. He had always been her favorite, the one among her children whom she considered least able to stand on his own two feet. It was just like Paul to have gone blustering off to San Francisco instead of remaining in County Tipperary. It was just like Kitty to have married a useless man. "There's not a girl in the town who'd touch him," she'd said to her daughter at the time, but Kitty had been headstrong and adamant, and there was Myles, doing nothing whatsoever except cleaning other people's windows for a pittance and placing bets in Donovan's, the turf accountant's. It was the shop and the arrangement Kitty had with Francis and her mother that kept up Kitty and her children, three of whom had already left the town, which in Mrs. Daly's opinion they mightn't have done if they'd had a better type of father. Mrs. Daly often wondered what her own two babies who'd died might have grown into, and imagined that they might have been like Francis, about whom she'd never had a moment's worry. Not in a million years would he give you the feeling that he was too big for his boots, the way Paul sometimes did with his lavishness and his talk of America. Francis wasn't silly like Kitty, or so sinful you couldn't forgive him, the way you couldn't forgive Edna, even though she was dead and buried in Toronto.

Francis understood how his mother felt about the family. She'd had a hard life, left a widow early on, trying to do the best she could for everyone. In turn, he did his best to compensate for the struggles and disappointments she'd suffered, cheering her in the evenings while Kitty and Myles and the youngest of their children watched the television in the kitchen. His mother had ignored Myles for ten years, ever since the day he'd taken money out of the till to pick up the odds on Gusty Spirit at Phoenix Park. And although Francis got on well enough with Myles, he quite understood that there should be a long aftermath to that day. There'd been a terrible row in the kitchen—Kitty screaming at Myles and Myles telling lies and Francis trying to keep them calm, saying they'd give the old woman a heart attack.

She didn't like upsets of any kind. All during the year before he was to visit the Holy Land, Francis read the New Testament to her in order to prepare her. He talked to her about Bethlehem and Nazareth and the miracles of the loaves and the fishes and all the other miracles. She kept nodding, but he often wondered if she didn't assume that he was casually referring to episodes in the Bible. As a child he had listened to such talk himself, with awe and fascination, imagining the walking on the water and the temptation in the wilderness. He had imagined the Cross carried to Calvary, and the rock rolled back from the tomb, and the rising from the dead on the third day. That he was now to be in such places seemed extraordinary to him, and he wished that his mother was younger so she could appreciate his good fortune and share it with him when she received the postcards he intended to send her every day. But her eyes seemed always to tell him that he was making a mistake, that somehow he was making a fool of himself by doing such a showy thing as going to the Holy Land. "I have the whole itinerary mapped out," his brother wrote from San Francisco. "There's nothing we'll miss."

It was the first time Francis had been in an airplane. He flew by Aer Lingus from Dublin to London and then changed to an El Al flight to Tel Aviv, where he was to meet Father Paul. He was nervous and he found the journey exhausting. All the time he seemed to be eating, and it was strange being among so many people he didn't know. "You will taste honey such as never before," an Israeli businessman in the seat next to his on the airplane assured him. "And Galilean figs. Make certain to taste Galilean figs." Make certain, too, the businessman said, to experience Jersualem by night and at dawn. He urged Francis to see places he had never heard of: the Yad Va-Shem, the treasures of the Shrine of the Book. He urged him to honor the martyrs of Masada and to learn a few words of Hebrew as a token of respect. He told him of a shop where he could buy mementos and warned him against Arab street traders.

"The hard case," Father Paul said, embracing Francis at the Tel Aviv airport. Father Paul had had a drink or two, and he suggested another when they arrived at the Plaza Hotel in Jerusalem. It was half past nine in the evening. "A quick little nightcap," Father Paul insisted, "and then hop into bed with you, Francis." They sat in an enormous open lounge with low, round tables and square modern armchairs. Father Paul told Francis it was the bar.

They had said what had to be said in the car from Tel Aviv to Jerusalem. Father Paul had asked about their mother, and Kitty and Myles. He'd asked about other people in the town—old Canon Mahon and Sergeant Malone. He and Father Steigmuller had had a great year of it, he reported: as well as everything else, the boys' home had turned out two tip-top football players. "We'll start on a tour at half-nine in the morning," he said. "I'll be sitting having breakfast at eight."

Francis went to bed, and Father Paul ordered another whiskey, with ice. To his great disappointment there was no Irish whiskey in the hotel, so he was having to content himself with Haig. He fell into conversation with an

American couple, making them promise that if they were ever in Ireland they wouldn't miss out County Tipperary. At eleven o'clock the barman said he was wanted at the reception desk, and when Father Paul went upstairs and announced himself he was given a message in an envelope. It was a telegram that had come, the girl said in poor English. Then she shook her head, saying it was a telex. He opened the envelope and learned that their mother had died.

Francis fell asleep immediately and dreamed that he was a boy again, out fishing with a friend whose identity he couldn't remember now.

On the telephone Father Paul ordered whiskey and ice to be brought to his room. Before drinking it, he took his jacket off and knelt by his bed to pray for his mother's salvation. When he'd completed the prayers, he walked slowly up and down the length of the room, occasionally sipping at his whiskey. He argued with himself and finally arrived at a decision.

For breakfast they had scrambled eggs that looked like yellow ice cream, and orange juice that was delicious. Francis asked about bacon, but Father Paul said that bacon was not readily available in Israel.

"Did you sleep all right?" Father Paul inquired. "Did you have the jet lag?"

"Jet lag?"

"A tiredness you get after jet flights. It'd knock you out for days."

"Ah, I slept great, Paul."

"Good man."

They lingered over breakfast. Father Paul reported a little more of what had happened in his parish during the year—in particular about the two young football players from the boys' home. Francis told about the decline in the cooking at Mrs. Shea's boarding house, as related to him by the three Christian Brothers. "I have a car laid on," Father Paul said, and twenty minutes later they walked out into the Jerusalem sunshine.

The hired car stopped on the way to the walls of the old city. It drew into a lay-by at Father Paul's request, and the two men got out and looked across a wide valley, dotted with houses and olive trees. A road curled along the distant slope opposite. "The Mount of Olives," Father Paul said. "And that's the road to Jericho." He pointed more particularly. "You see there, that group of eight big olives?" he said. "Just off the road, where the church is?"

Francis thought he did but was not sure. There were so many olive trees, and there was more than one church.

"The Garden of Gethsemane," Father Paul said.

Francis did not say anything. He continued to gaze at the distant church with the clump of olive trees beside it. Wild flowers were profuse on the slopes of the valley—smears of orange and blue on land that looked poor. Two Arab women herded goats.

"Could we see it closer?" he asked, and his brother said that definitely they would. They returned to the waiting car, and Father Paul ordered it to the Gate of St. Stephen.

Tourists heavy with cameras thronged the Via Dolorosa. Brown, barefoot children asked for alms. Stallkeepers pressed their different goods: cotton dresses, metalware, mementos, sacred objects. "Get out of the way," Father Paul kept saying to them, genially laughing to show he wasn't being abrupt. Francis wanted to stand still and close his eyes, to visualize for a moment the carrying of the Cross. But the ceremony of the Stations, familiar to him for as long as he could remember, seemed unreal. Try as he would, Christ's journey refused to enter his imagination, and his own plain church seemed closer to the heart of the matter than the noisy lane he was now being jostled on. "God damn it, of course it's genuine," an angry American voice proclaimed, in reply to another voice, which insisted that cheating had taken place. The voices argued about a piece of wood, neat beneath plastic in a little box—a sample or not of the Cross that had been carried.

They arrived at the Church of the Holy Sepulchre, and at the Chapel of the Nailing to the Cross, where they prayed. They passed through the Chapel of the Angel, to the tomb of Christ. Nobody spoke in the marble cell, but when they left the church Francis overheard a quiet man with spectacles saying it was unlikely that a body would have been buried within the walls of the city. They walked to Hezekiah's Pool and out of the Old City at the Jaffa Gate, where their hired car was waiting for them.

"Are you peckish?" Father Paul asked, and although Francis said he wasn't, they returned to the hotel.

"DELAY FUNERAL TILL MONDAY" was the telegram Father Paul had sent. There was an early flight on Sunday, in time for an afternoon one from London to Dublin. With luck there would be a late train on Sunday evening, and if there wasn't they'd have to fix a car. That would give them four and a half days. "FUNERAL ELEVEN MONDAY," the telegram at the reception desk confirmed. "Ah, isn't that great?" said Father Paul to himself, crumpling the telegram.

"Will we have a small one?" he suggested in the open area that was the bar. "Or better still a big one." He laughed. He was in good spirits in spite of the death that had taken place. He gestured at the barman, wagging his head and smiling jovially.

His pink face had reddened in the morning sun; there were specks of sweat on his forehead and his nose. "Bethlehem this afternoon," he laid down. "Unless the jet lag—?"

"I haven't got the jet lag."

In the Nativity Boutique, Francis bought for his mother a small metal plate with a fish on it. He had stood for a moment—scarcely able to believe it—on the spot where the manger had been, in the Church of the Nativity. As in the Via Dolorosa, it had been difficult to clear his mind of the surroundings that crowded in: the exotic Greek Orthodox trappings, the foreign-looking priests, the Oriental smell. Gold, frankincense, and myrrh, he'd kept thinking—for somehow the church seemed more the church of the Three Kings than of Joseph and Mary and their child. Afterward they returned to Jerusalem—to the Tomb of the Virgin and the Garden of Gethsemane. "It could have been anywhere," he heard the quiet, bespectacled man from the Church of the Holy Sepulchre remark in Gethsemane. "They're only guessing."

Father Paul rested in the late afternoon, lying down on his bed with his jacket off. He slept from half past five until quarter past seven and awoke refreshed. He picked up the telephone and asked for whiskey and ice, and when it arrived he undressed and had a bath, relaxing in the warm water with the drink on a ledge in the tiled wall beside him. There would be time to take in Nazareth and Galilee. He was particularly keen that his brother should see Galilee, because Galilee had atmosphere and was beautiful. There wasn't, in his own opinion, very much to Nazareth, but it would be a pity to miss it all the same. It was at the Sea of Galilee that he intended to tell his brother of their mother's death.

"We've had a great day," Francis wrote on a postcard that showed an aerial view of Jerusalem. "The Church of the Holy Sepulchre, where Our Lord's tomb is, and Gethsemane and Bethlehem. Paul's in great form." He addressed it to his mother, and then wrote other cards, to Kitty and Myles, and to the three Christian Brothers at Mrs. Shea's, and to Canon Mahon. He gave thanks that he was privileged to be in Jerusalem. He read St. Mark and some of St. Matthew. He said his Rosary.

"Will we chance the wine?" Father Paul said at dinner—not that wine was something he went in for, but a waiter had come up and put a large padded wine list into his hand.

"Ah, no, no," Francis protested, but already Father Paul was running his eye down the list.

"Have you local wine?" he inquired of the waiter. "A nice red one?"

The waiter nodded and hurried away, and Francis hoped he wouldn't get drunk—red wine on top of the whiskey he'd had in the bar before the meal. He'd only had the one whiskey, not being much used to it, and made it last through his brother's three.

"I heard some boyos in the bar," Father Paul said, "making a great song and dance about the local red wine."

Wine made Francis think of the Holy Communion, but he didn't say so. He said the soup was delicious, and he drew his brother's attention to a custom in the hotel—a porter ringing a bell and walking about with a person's name chalked on a little blackboard on the end of a rod.

"It's a way of paging you," Father Paul explained. "Isn't it nicer than bellowing out some fellow's name?" He smiled his easy smile, his eyes beginning to water as a result of the drinks he'd had. He was beginning to feel a strain: he kept thinking of their mother lying there, of what she'd say if she knew what he'd done, how she'd savagely upbraid him for keeping the fact from Francis. Out of duty and humanity he had returned each year to see her, because, after all, you only had the one mother. But he had never cared for her.

Francis went for a walk after dinner. There were young soldiers on the streets with what seemed to be toy guns, but he knew that the guns were real. In the shopwindows there were television sets for sale, and furniture and clothes, just like anywhere else. There were advertisments for some film or other—two writhing women without a stitch on them, the kind of thing you wouldn't see in Country Tipperary. "You want something sir?" a girl said, smiling at him with broken front teeth. The siren of a police car or an ambulance shrilled urgently nearby. He shook his head at the girl. "No, I don't want anything," he said, and then realized what she had meant. She was small and very dark, no more than a child. He hurried on, praying for her.

When he returned to the hotel, he found his brother in the lounge with other people, two men and two women. Father Paul was ordering a round of drinks and called out to the barman to bring an extra whiskey. "Ah, no, no," Francis protested, anxious to go to his room and to think about the day, to read the New Testament, and perhaps to write a few more postcards. Music was coming from speakers that could not be seen.

"My brother, Francis," Father Paul said to the people he was with, and the people all gave their names, adding that they came from New York. "I was telling them about Tipp," Father Paul said to his brother, offering his packet of cigarettes around.

"You like Jerusalem, Francis?" one of the American women asked him, and he replied that he hadn't been able to take it in yet. Then, feeling that he didn't sound enthusiastic enough, he added that being there was the experience of a lifetime.

Father Paul went on talking about County Tipperary and then spoke of his parish in San Francisco, the boys' home and the two promising football players, the plans for the new church. The Americans listened, and in a moment the conversation drifted on to the subject of their travels in England, their visits to Istanbul and Athens, an argument they'd had at customs in Tel Aviv. "Well, I'm ready to hit the hay," one of the men announced eventually, standing up.

The others stood up, too, and so did Francis. Father Paul remained where he was, gesturing again in the direction of the barman. "Sit down for a nightcap," he urged his brother.

"Ah, no, no—" Francis began.

"Bring us two more of those," the priest ordered abruptly, and the barman hurried away. "Listen," said Father Paul. "I've something to tell you."

After dinner, while Francis had been out on his walk, before Father Paul had got into conversation with the Americans, he had said to himself that he couldn't stand the strain. It was the old woman stretched out above the hardware shop, already stiff as a board, with the little lights burning in her room: he kept seeing all that, as if she wanted him to, as if she were trying to haunt him. He didn't think he could go on—nice as the idea was—with what he'd planned, with waiting until they got up to Galilee.

Francis didn't want to drink any more. He hadn't wanted the whiskey that his brother had ordered for him earlier, nor the one the Americans had ordered for him. He didn't want the one that the barman was bringing. He thought he'd just leave it there, hoping his brother wouldn't see it. He lifted the glass to his lips, but he managed not to drink any.

"A bad thing has happened," Father Paul said.

"Bad? How do you mean, Paul?"

"Are you ready for it?" He paused. Then he said, "She died."

Francis didn't know what he was talking about. He didn't know who was meant to be dead, or why his brother was behaving in an odd manner. He didn't like to think it, but he had to: His brother wasn't fully sober.

"Our mother died," Father Paul said. "I'm after getting a telegram."

The huge area that was the lounge of the Plaza Hotel, the endless tables and people sitting at them, the swiftly moving waiters and barmen—Francis saw them with a feeling that he was not where he appeared to be, that he wasn't sitting with his brother, who was wiping his lips with a handkerchief. In his confusion he thought for a moment that he was struggling his way up the Via Dolorosa again, and then that he was in the Nativity Boutique.

"Take it easy, boy," his brother was saying. "Take a mouthful of whiskey."

Francis didn't obey that injunction. He asked his brother to repeat what he had said before, and Father Paul repeated that their mother had died.

Francis closed his eyes and tried as well to shut away the sounds around them. He prayed for the salvation of his mother's soul. "Blessed Virgin, intercede," his own voice said in his mind. "Dear Mary, let her few small sins be forgiven."

Having rid himself of his secret, Father Paul felt instant relief. With the best of intentions, he had been foolish to think he could maintain the secret until they arrived in a place that was perhaps the most suitable in the world for hearing of the death of a person close to you. He took a gulp of his whiskey and wiped his mouth with his handkerchief again. He watched his brother, waiting for his eyes to open.

"When did it happen?" Francis asked eventually.

"Yesterday."

"And the telegram only came—"

"It came last night, Francis. I wanted to save you the pain."

"Save me? How could you save me? I sent her a postcard, Paul."

"Listen to me, Francis—"

"How could you save me the pain?"

"I wanted to tell you when we got up to Galilee."

Francis couldn't understand his brother: he couldn't understand what he meant by saying a telegram had come last night, why at a moment like this he was talking about Galilee. He didn't know why they were sitting in this noisy place when they should be back in Ireland.

"I fixed the funeral for Monday," Father Paul said.

Francis nodded, not grasping the significance of this arrangement. "We'll be back there this time tomorrow," he said.

"No need for that, Francis. Sunday morning's time enough."

"But she's dead—"

"We'll be there in time for the funeral."

"We can't stay here if she's dead."

It was this, Father Paul realized, that he'd been afraid of when he'd argued with himself and made his plan. If he'd knocked on Francis's door the night before, Francis would have wanted to return immediately without seeing a single stone of the land he had come so far to be moved by.

"We could go straight up to Galilee in the

morning." Father Paul said quietly. "You'll find comfort in Galilee, Francis."

But Francis shook his head. "I want to be with her," he said.

Father Paul lighted a cigarette. He nodded at a hovering waiter, indicating his need of another drink. He said to himself that he must keep his cool—an expression he was fond of. "Take it easy, Francis," he said.

"Is there a plane out in the morning? Can we make arrangements now?" Francis looked about him as if for a member of the hotel staff who might be helpful.

"No good will be done by tearing off home, Francis. What's wrong with Sunday?"

"I want to be with her."

Anger swelled within Father Paul. If he began to argue, his words would become slurred: he knew that from experience. He must keep his cool and speak slowly and clearly, making a few simple points. It was typical of her, he thought, to die inconveniently.

"You've come all this way," he said as slowly as he could without sounding peculiar. "Why cut it any shorter than we need? We'll be losing a week anyway. She wouldn't want us to go back."

"I think she would."

He was right in that. Her possessiveness in her lifetime would have reached out across a dozen continents for Francis. She'd known what she was doing by dying when she had.

"I shouldn't have come," Francis said. "She didn't want me to come."

"You're thirty-seven years of age, Francis."

"I did wrong to come."

"You did no such thing."

The time he'd taken her to Rome, she'd been difficult for the whole week—complaining about the food, saying everywhere was dirty. Whenever he'd spent anything, she'd disapproved. All his life, Father Paul felt, he'd done his best for her. He had told her before anyone else when he'd decided to enter the priesthood, certain that she'd be pleased. "I thought you'd take over the shop," she'd said.

"What difference could it make to wait, Francis?"

"There's nothing to wait for."

As long as he lived, Francis knew, he would never forgive himself. As long as he lived, he would say to himself that he hadn't been able to wait a few years, until she'd passed quietly on. He might even have been in the room with her when it happened.

"It was a terrible thing not to tell me," he said. "I sat down and wrote her a postcard, Paul. I bought her a plate."

"So you said."

"You're drinking too much of that whiskey."

"Now, Francis, don't be silly."

"You're half drunk and she's lying there."

"She can't be brought back, no matter what we do."

"She never hurt anyone," Francis said.

Father Paul didn't deny that, although it wasn't true. She had hurt their sister Kitty, constantly reproaching her for marrying Myles, long after Kitty had seen it was a mistake. She'd driven Edna to Canada when Edna, still unmarried, had a miscarriage that only the family knew about. She had made a shadow out of Francis, although Francis didn't know it. Having failed to hold on to her other children, she had grasped her last-born to her, as if she had borne him to destroy him.

"It'll be you who'll say a Mass for her?" Francis said.

"Yes, of course it will."

"You should have told me."

Francis realized why, all day, he'd been disappointed. From the moment when the hired car had pulled into the lay-by and his brother had pointed across the valley at the Garden of Gethsemane, he'd been disappointed and had not admitted it. He'd been disappointed in the Via Dolorosa and in the Church of the Holy Sepulchre and in Bethlehem. He remembered the bespeckled man who'd kept saying that you couldn't be sure about anything. All the people with cameras made it impossible to think, all the jostling and pushing was distracting. When he'd said there was too much to take in, he'd meant something different.

"Her death got in the way," he said.

"What do you mean, Francis?"

"It didn't feel like Jerusalem, it didn't feel like Bethlehem."

"But it is, Francis, it is."

"There are soldiers with guns all over the place. And a girl came up to me on the street. There was that man with a bit of the Cross. There's you, drinking and smoking in this place—"

"Now, listen to me, Francis—"

"Nazareth would be a disappointment. And the Sea of Galilee. And the Church of the Loaves and Fishes." His voice had risen. He lowered it. "I couldn't believe in the Stations this morning. I couldn't see it happening the way I do at home."

"That's nothing to do with her death, Francis. You've got a bit of jet lag, you'll settle yourself up in Galilee. There's an atmosphere in Galilee that nobody misses."

"I'm not going near Galilee." He struck the surface of the table, and Father Paul told him to contain himself. People turned their heads, aware that anger had erupted in the pale-faced man with the priest.

"Quieten up," Father Paul commanded

sharply, but Francis didn't.

"She knew I was making a fool of myself, a man out of a shop trying to be big—"

"Will you keep your voice down? Of course you're not making a fool of yourself."

"Will you find out about planes tomorrow morning?"

Father Paul sat for a moment longer, not saying anything, hoping his brother would say he was sorry. Naturally it was a shock, naturally he'd be emotional and feel guilty; in a moment it would be better. But it wasn't, and Francis didn't say he was sorry. Instead he began to weep.

"Let's go up to your room," Father Paul said, "and I'll fix about the plane."

Francis nodded but did not move. His sobbing ceased, and then he said, "I'll always hate the Holy Land now."

"No need for that, Francis."

But Francis felt there was, and he felt he would hate, as well, the brother he had admired for as long as he could remember. In the lounge of the Plaza Hotel he felt mockery surfacing everywhere. His brother's deceit, and the endless whiskey in his brother's glass, and his brother's casualness after a death seemed like a scorning of the Church that honored so steadfastly the mother of its founder. Vivid in his mind, his own mother's eyes had told him he was making a mistake and upbraided him for not heeding her.

Of course there was a mockery everywhere—in the splinter of the wood beneath plastic, and the soldiers with guns that were not toys, and the writhing nakedness in the Holy City. He'd become part of it himself, sending postcards to the dead. Not speaking again to his brother, he went to his room to pray.

"Eight in the morning, sir," the girl at the reception desk said, and Father Paul asked that arrangements be made to book two seats on the plane, explaining that it was an emergency, that a death had occurred. "It will be all right, sir," the girl promised.

He went slowly downstairs to the bar. He sat in a corner and lighted a cigarette and ordered two whiskeys and ice, as if expecting a companion. He drank them both himself and ordered two more. Francis would return to County Tipperary, and after the funeral he would take up again the life she had ordained for him. In his brown cotton coat he would serve customers with nails and hinges and wire. He would regularly go to Mass and to Confession and to Men's Confraternity. He would sit alone in the lace-curtained sitting room, lonely for the woman who had made him what he was.

Father Paul lighted a fresh cigarette from the end of his previous one. He continued to order whiskey in two glasses. Already he could sense the hatred that Francis had earlier felt taking root in himself. He wondered if he would ever again return in July to County Tipperary, and imagined that he would not.

At midnight he rose to make the journey to bed and found himself unsteady on his feet. People looked at him, thinking it disgraceful for a priest to be drunk in Jerusalem, with cigarette ash all over his clerical clothes.

A QUESTION OF DEGREE

by Charles Healy

MONSIGNOR CAREY, dozing in a red, imitation-leather chair in his room, jumped awake so sharply that his breviary slipped from his lap to the floor. Rubbing his eyes, he looked slowly about the room as if he had not fully expected to see it again; past seventy and of uneven health, he knew that even a cat nap could easily stretch into eternity. Thus he never went to sleep without his breviary or beads at hand, determined, as it were, to die with his boots on. He hoped, in fact, that by so arranging himself (as if God were susceptible to the power of suggestion), he would insure that he would die quietly and painlessly in his sleep.

Monsignor sincerely mourned the death of any of his friends, but he could not help taking some secret consolation in their passing. Though his faith was unshakeable, he did not feel any overwhelming confidence in eternity, for he simply could not imagine millions upon millions of centuries of endless variety, painless and beautiful. There were occasions, in fact, when, if the choice were put to him, he would have chosen oblivion over heaven, although in his heart he knew that it would be as promised, and he would be grateful. In the meantime, he would console himself with the fact that so many of his friends had preceded him and would cushion his own fall into paradise.

This line of thought reminded him of the dream from which he had just awakened. In it he had died and gone to heaven. Now he remembered the bitterness and keen disappointment he had felt because the paradise for which he had striven for seven decades was not, as he had so often assured the faithful, beyond finite imaginings. It was, in fact, exactly as it had been pictured in countless movies: an infinity of swirling, calf-deep fog.

Since one direction was much the same as any other, he had walked ahead without purpose, keeping his eyes down lest he step through a ragged hole in the clouds. When he looked up, he was in front of a tall figure dressed in immaculate robes and seated on a golden throne. Like a drunk who cannot lift his eyes above a person's neck and so addresses himself to the knot of their tie, as if it were a microphone, Monsignor found himself unable to look any higher than the man's silken beard. He sensed, however, that the man was smiling kindly, just as he sensed that several figures standing around the throne were not.

Monsignor studied the several sandaled feet intently, while he cast about in his mind for something to say. Any number of appropriate

Scripture quotations came to mind, but he rejected them as presumptuous. He had decided on paraphrase as a way of making Biblical small talk to get over the initial awkwardness, and was about to open with, "I understand your house has many mansions," when he realized that he was carrying a collection basket which was overflowing with budget envelopes and large bills. The basket was so light it seemed that even the smaller envelopes of the children must be stuffed with bills (or, he thought for one terrible moment, empty). This was a demonstration so untypical of his parishioners that he thought they must have somehow known that this time the money would be delivered directly, not detoured over unsearchable roads of church repairs, lay teachers' salaries or fuel oil for the convent. As he stepped happily forward and extended the basket on its long handle to the man on the throne, Monsignor forgave his parishioners their former niggardliness and even resolved to send a few miracles their way: a healing spring, perhaps that would bubble through the blacktop of the church parking lot some Sunday morning just as the eleven let out.

His hands were starting to perspire, and he was afraid that, light as it was, the basket would slip from his grasp. Why hadn't He taken it? Wasn't it enough? Monsignor knew he was not all angel yet, for he very nearly gave the basket an impatient shake and might have if he had not heard the sound of heavy jingling as if of ancient coins. When he looked up he saw that the long, slender hand which had lain so lightly on the arm of the throne was fishing about in the folds of his robes. *He was digging for money!* Apparently He thought that it was a collection rather than an offering. Monsignor's mouth worked wildly, but no sound came. The figures around the throne, without actually doing anything, had become menacing when the sound of his breviary slapping the floor woke Monsignor.

Though he had dozed for just a few minutes, the dream seemed so long that he was surprised to see that it was still light outside. He squinted at the clock on the dresser. It was well outside the clear-cut circle of his vision, so he reached into the inside pocket of his cassock for the glasses which, their stems folded under like the legs of a yoga, were sitting on the dresser in front of the clock.

As he brought his hand out of his cassock, Monsignor noticed in the palm a smudge of red. He held his hand close to his face and squinted at it, amazed. Could it be? After a moment he held up the other hand. It too, it seemed, was bloody. Monsignor dropped his hands, palms up, to his lap. He was as exhausted by the discovery as if he had done some strenuous exercise.

It was significant of Monsignor's personality that he accepted the fact of the stigmata so quickly. He was a practical man, an administrator, always had been. He began his ministry in the chancery and had remained there—through three bishops—until he had been given this parish, a choice plum. As a pastor, he remained as distant and mysterious as he had been in his former position, moving quietly through the corridors on such small steps, the skirt of his cassock exhaling behind him, that he seemed to be on wheels. He was like a celebrity in his own parish: everyone knew who he was, but he knew practically no one. The two curates served as his subtitles: "The Monsignor says you can use the church hall for the meeting Thursday night," Father Fonda would say, standing in the rear of the church between Monsignor and one of the parishioners. Only a desire not to embarrass the curate and make him more truly the man in the middle kept the parishioner from acidly replying, "Will you tell the Monsignor I said thanks?"

Only once, shortly after he had come to St. John's, did Monsignor attempt to break the mold and become, to some extent, a "people's priest." Seeking a safe area of contact with his new flock, he had decided on their children. He knew that the smallest smile aimed at a child was enough to satisfy the parents that its author was a person of warmth and discernment, and they would not ask for more. Indeed, Monsignor had often seen a whole roomful of intelligent company rendered speechless, or, at the very least, incoherent, by the insertion of a child into its center.

So, Monsignor took to kissing babies. His bent, bussing figure at the rear of the church on Sunday mornings became as familiar as the holy water font. But the practice ended as suddenly as it had begun.

One Sunday morning, Mrs. Robert Allen, the mother of five, arrived for Mass with her small brood. The first four children filed past Monsignor, each receiving a kiss. Mrs. Allen, who had been making last minute adjustments in all the children's outfits right up to the door of the church, brought up the rear with Marjorie, her youngest. Intent on tying Marjorie's pinafore and being in a position similar to Monsignor's, she turned absent-mindedly when she came opposite him and planted a quick kiss on his cheek.

Though there were only three witnesses to the incident and though their discretion was unimpeachable, Monsignor was never again seen in the rear of the church in any but an upright position. An experienced spiritual tracker, he read the kiss as sign that higher powers disapproved. In later years, when the mere mention of the name of Monsignor Joseph Dineen was enough to send groups of clergy into gales of laughter, Monsignor Carey found himself almost grateful for Marie Allen's kiss.

Monsignor Dineen, whose parish was in the northwest tip of the diocese, had initiated a similar practice in his church years before. He, too, kept a faithful Sunday morning vigil during which he kissed the little girls and patted the small boys on the head as they passed. Unfortunately, as the children advanced in age, Monsignor Dineen advanced in senility, and didn't realize that the children were now grown. Thus he could be seen each Sunday happily and scandalously embracing nubile young ladies. Some of the younger priests were fond of speculating on Monsignor Dineen's eventual funeral. They painted it as a Rudolph Valentino affair with hundreds of young Catholic ladies throwing themselves on the casket, then withdrawing weakly to the convent. All but one: a silent, striking beauty in basic black who would appear at the cemetery each year and lay a mysterious white envelope with black lettering on his tomb. On closer inspection, the envelope would be found to read, "Annual Collection."

So Monsignor, the practical priest, accepted the stigmata in his own peculiarly philsophical way. He did not worry about the fact that no wounds crouched in hideous beauty under the blood, for he vaguely remembered from his Lives of the Saints that they sometimes appeared gradually in the beginning, coming and going at certain intervals, usually every Friday. He wondered about his worthiness, but decided that no one was really worthy to wear the stigmata, and so it became a question of the degree of unworthiness, whether he was less unworthy than another. Of course, there was the possibility that the choice was not made entirely for spiritual reasons. For example, from a physical or geographical viewpoint, Monsignor was the obvious choice. His parish was centrally located with plenty of hotels and restaurants to accommodate the thousands of pilgrims who would inevitably and endlessly come. On Sundays, he was sure they would be given the use of the municipal parking lot which ordinarily stood all but empty on that day. Now, if Father Coleman, for example, had been selected to bear the stigmata, the situation would have been quite different. His parish was on the east side of town where the streets were narrow and twisting and, at certain hours of the day, gagged with grocery carts. There were no hotels to speak of and most of the restaurants were of the greasy spoon variety. Monsignor Carey concluded that, if the choice had been up to him, he would have had to choose himself.

Relieved, he pushed himself out of the chair and started for the bathroom. He kicked his breviary, and it shot across the room ahead of him, scattering holy cards. He picked them up, replaced them in the breviary, placed the breviary on the bookcase, then stepped into the bathroom.

It was not until the last of the red liquid had swirled out of sight that he realized he was washing a first-class relic down the drain. Well, there would be plenty more where that came from, he throught grimly.

Monsignor returned to the bedroom, and, hearing voices outside, moved to the window. As he watched his two curates walking over from the church where they had been hearing confessions, it occurred to Monsignor that he would soon be hearing confessions again, for people were known to travel incredible distances, often on foot and in all sorts of weather, to receive spiritual advice from a stigmatist. His shoulders drooped. He frankly hated hearing confessions and had not, in fact, heard any since he had become a pastor—unless you were to count the few times he had happened on an accident or made an ill-timed visit to the hospital. (Sometimes, walking into the hospital rooms of parishioners who had been reported "doing nicely" and finding them clinging to life with a much fainter grip than the one they quickly fixed on his arm, he wondered if someone was pulling his leg.) He realized that it would not look good if, after the stigmata had become permanent and public, word got around that he hadn't heard confessions in years. Not that he was remiss. As pastor, it was his privilege to hear confessions or not. But at the same time, it was his duty, where possible, to avoid scandal, even unjust scandal. Perhaps that was why the wounds were not yet permanent: to give him time to get back into harness. It was something to think about. A short time later, thinking about it, he went down to dinner.

Monsignor stood at the head of the table, the plates stacked in front of him. The tip of the carving knife appeared, disappeared and reappeared at the side of the roast like a silver serpent's tongue. One by one the slices of red meat slumped and piled on the platter. Monsignor placed several slices on each dish, added a portion of potatoes and vegetables and passed one to each of his curates.

When they had finished their dinner, Monsignor rang the bell to summon the cook. The bell was a mate to the one used at Mass, and Father Dennis, the younger of the two curates, could not hear it rung without hearing an invisible congregation sliding wearily to its knees. Conversely, when the bell was rung during his

Mass, he saw, instead of the host or chalice which he held elevated over his head, Monsignor sitting at the dinner table absently twisting one of the red buttons of his cassock as if it were a control knob with which he was trying to tune in Rome.

Esther slammed into the dining room without ceremony, employing the same heavy tread which formerly was responsible for the spasmodic jumping of the television picture in the priests' study. They had uncovered this fact one night by carrying out a plan of Monsignor's. Monsignor sat in the study in front of the television, Father Fonda was stationed on the second floor at the head of the stairs and Father Dennis stood nervously outside Esther's room at the rear of the house. When he heard her leap out of the chair and start across the room to exchange a *Look* for a *Life* from a library of such literature on her bureau, he signaled to Father Fonda, who called to Monsignor, who reported to them when they returned to the study that the television had indeed gone haywire at precisely that time. Monsignor, who was the first to point the finger of suspicion at Esther, was so pleased that they had solved the problem—the repair man had been summoned three times and had finally laid the blame on fallout—he called for sherry all around. They were on their second glass when it occured to Father Dennis, who had been feeling giddy right after the first glass, that the incident was not unlike the gospel in which a rich man returns home from seeing Christ and finds that the fever left his dying son at the very moment the man himself was speaking to Christ. He was about to share this intuition with the others when the television began to act up again, and they realized that they had uncovered the cause of their trouble but not the cure. This last was eventually accomplished by presenting Esther with a new radio, a phonograph and a television set (with, of course, remote control). Although these did not have the intended effect of keeping Esther in her seat, they did so clutter her tiny room that a trip to the bureau now required a series of sharp turns and detours which precluded any of her long, heavy steps.

Rather than walk around the table, Esther leaned over as far as she could, then tossed Father Dennis' jello dish the last few inches so that the dish spun around like a coin before coming to rest. For Esther, this was a minor offense. When she was in a hurry to get out in the evening (to where, God could only guess), she would carry their plates away before they were finished and, if they lingered over dessert and coffee, she would turn the dining-room lights on and off like a nun signaling the end of a high school dance. On the other hand, when she had time to kill, she would hover about the table rearranging serving dishes suggestively and urging them to "clean up" everything. "Wanna finish these?" she would ask, holding the potato dish over one of their plates, the serving spoon cocked. If anyone hesitated—plop!—the potatoes landed on his plate and Esther wheeled and marched triumphant to the kitchen, her great buttocks alternately punching at her dress like two doomed cats.

For something which fought so desperately to get off the spoon, the jello was remarkably docile once inside the mouth, allowing itself to be strained repeatedly through the teeth until it was restored to its original liquid state and swallowed. This process was occupying the attention of the two curates when Monsignor announced, "I'll take confessions tonight."

Both priests were understandably alarmed; Monsignor's delinquency in the matter of hearing confessions was a favorite topic of conversation. They had, in fact, been discussing it earlier when they noticed that he was watching them from his bedroom window. Now, looking at each other in surprise, they wondered if he could have heard them, although, given the distance and Monsignor's imperfect hearing, this seemed impossible. On the other hand, it now appeared that nothing was impossible.

"What?" said Father Fonda, needing time to think.

"I said I'll take confessions," Monsignor snapped back. "You two can decide whose box I'll take."

"Whose box?" Father Fonda repeated, needing more time.

"Well, I don't have any place to go," said Father Dennis.

"Neither do I," said Father Fonda quickly.

"Then stay home!" Monsignor said. "What's the problem?" With that he pushed his chair back and left the room. The two priests looked at each other, shrugged, and went after him.

They found him in the study watching the television warm up, and took chairs on either side of him. At one time there had been a comfortable couch in the study, but one Saturday night Monsignor and Father Fonda were watching television with a visiting Jesuit when Father Fonda fell asleep and slumped over so that he was resting against Monsignor. Monsignor was barely able to budge him, and when he looked to the Jesuit for help he realized from the way he was frowning at the television that he was obviously trying not to look, as if he thought the curate went to sleep every night with his head on Monsignor's shoulder. A few days later the couch was replaced by two straight-backed chairs which the curates now occupied.

"They'll probably be pretty heavy tonight," Father Fonda said without looking away from the television.

"That's right," said Father Dennis. "That rain around four kept a lot away."

"Yeah, I got all my office said."

A little later Father Dennis offered, "Gee, that box is hot."

"And that seat is like a board."

Monsignor, feeling himself weakening, stood up, placed his collar around his neck, tucked in the goatee-like rabat, snapped the collar button and fled.

A little later, he stepped into the confessional with all the enthusiasm of someone putting on wet trousers. Before pulling the door to, he checked his equipment: the switch for the red light outside which indicated that there were no penitents inside (he hoped he would have occasion to use it); the arm-rests just below the screens on either side of him; the small ledges near the floor on which he could break the monotony for his feet. He took out his rosary beads, slowly unknotted them and let them dangle from his fingers. Then, unable to think of anything else to do, he leaned forward and closed the door, sealing himself in.

From the steady flow of penitents, Monsignor judged that Father Fonda, whose confessional he was seated in, was either a good confessor or an easy one. He decided he was the latter, because, as a rule, people didn't care for a "good" confessor; the admonitions and advice he offered kept them in the confessional too long and they knew what those succeeding them in line would think: the same things they themselves thought when someone stayed in the confessional for more than a few minutes.

Monsignor realized that if judged by this one stint, he too would be considered an easy confessor. He was too busy with his own thoughts (whenever his hands perspired, he held them in the strip of light which came in between the door and examined them just to be sure; he also worked his feet around to see if there was any pain or if his socks were wet and sticking to his feet) to say more than, "For your penance say three Our Fathers three Hail Marys make a Good Act of Contrition."

Around quarter to nine, when he was thinking of slipping out early, the sound of bones cracking told him that someone was in the confessional shifting from knee to knee to attract his attention. He shut off the light and pushed the slide back. Immediately a boy of about ten started rattling off his sins.

"Bless me father for I have sinned. This is three weeks since my last confession I accuse myself of. Talked during Mass three times, looked at magazines I shouldn't once. . . ."

As the boy droned on down his list of sins, real and otherwise (at one point he admitted "crossing against the light" and Monsignor made a mental note to have another talk with the nuns), Monsignor became aware of something—a breathing other than the penitent's. He squinted through the screen, but it was too dark.

"Who's there?" he asked.

The boy stopped speaking, but there was no answer.

"I said, who's there?"

"It's me, Father," answered a voice near his shoulder.

"Monsignor," corrected Monsignor.

"It's me, Monsignor."

"Who else?"

"Who else?"

"Who's with you? I know there's two of you."

There was a long pause.

"Well...?" Monsignor finally said.

"He's my friend, Father."

"Monsignor!"

"Monsignor."

"What's he doing here?"

"He's just listening."

"Listening! What do you mean listening?"

"He's not a Catholic like us."

Monsignor wisely abandoned questioning the penitent. That "us" told him the boy was prepared to come over to his side against his non-Catholic friend.

"What are you doing here?" Monsignor

asked. There was no answer at first, then there was a muffled sound as if one had punched the other.

"Nothin'." The second voice was behind and above the other and Monsignor felt an unreasonable anger that the boy was not even kneeling.

"*Nothing!*"

"I don' know. I just wanted to see what it was like. *He* said I could. . . ." Another punch, only harder.

"What's the matter with you?" Monsignor asked the lower darkness. "You can't bring people in here. Get out, both of you!"

"Yes, Father. . .*Monsignor!*" There were scuffling sounds as the two fought to get out, then a quick glimpse of light as the curtain was displaced and fell back.

As soon as they had gone, Monsignor remembered that he should have gotten their names—the Catholic boy's at least. In his anger, he had taken "It's me" as positive identification. He knew it was too late to catch them, but the sexton or someone might have seen them. Pulling himself to his feet, he opened the door and came face to face with Mrs. Whiteley.

Nora Whiteley, even at eighty-six, lived in constant fear that her voice would be recognized in the confessional. She was old enough and slowed enough to have the priest come to her home, but she had no intention of making it that easy for him. Instead, she made her way to church where she filtered her sins through a handkerchief and kept her head down because you could never be sure that priests, what with all those years of sitting in the dark, listening, hadn't developed a special sight. In Nora Whiteley's case, some of her fears were well founded: there was a distinctive crack in her voice which no number of handkerchiefs could disguise. This crack also identified her as the would-be anonymous voice which called the rectory periodically to keep the priests on the straight and narrow. She once called to tell Father Fonda that he was a wild, carefree man, unfit to wear the collar, and that he was sure to burn in hell for certain offenses which were never clearly defined. When he pressed to know who was calling, she said, "A friend," and hung up.

On another occasion, when she called to warn Father Dennis against sins of the flesh, he remembered that earlier that day, when he was driving several cheerleaders to the CYO basketball game, he had driven past Mrs. Whiteley's house. She must have seen him from the upstairs window where, taking advantage of the lace curtains which gave her a clear view of the street while making her invisible from outside, she kept an almost constant watch. Occasionally, Mrs. Whiteley did strike bone. This time, however, she had come quite wide of the mark.

When he was twelve years old, young Michael Dennis had had an unsolicited look up his aunt's dress as she fell heavily into a chair. He saw there, besides the flesh rising like bread above the stockings, such a complex of nylon, elastic and silk, that he thought, for her, dressing must have been like packing a parachute. (Did that long strap, when pulled, release all her undergarments so that they fell in folds at her feet?) It is just possible that at that moment, subconsciously, the future Father Dennis decided never to marry.

"Did you see them?" Monsignor asked Mrs. Whiteley, whose bright eyes glared at him over her handkerchief.

"What's that?"

"There were two of them," Monsignor said, turning hopelessly back to the confessional. He knew that she could not have seen them, for she would have been walking with her head down, searching the near darkness with eyes and stick. She stood leaning on her cane like a golfer waiting for her partner to take his shot, staring after him.

Monsignor allowed her enough time to get into the confessional, then opened the slide. He saw her silhouetted at the entrance holding the curtain aside. For a long moment they stared at each other. Finally, Mrs. Whiteley hissed, "Peeping Tom!" dropped the curtain and moved away.

Back at the rectory, Monsignor looked into the study where Father Dennis, who had finished confessions before him, was watching television.

Monsignor placed one hand on the door jamb and let it take his weight. "Who's got the sermon tomorrow?" he asked.

"Bob has."

"Tell him I'll take it." He turned away, then stopped and turned half way back. "And ask him to bring the announcement book up to my room." He ignored Father Dennis' amazed expression.

Upstairs, he climbed into his pajamas and then into bed. He picked up a book he had been reading but could not bring himself to open it. Lying there, he fiddled with one of the buttons on his silk pajama shirt, letting his mind wander. He wondered if the buttons were made so large to make it easier to operate them when you were tired. He remembered reading somewhere that if you were lost on the desert you could suck moisture out of a button. If that were true then, as buttons go, one of those on his pajama shirt would be equivalent to a tall glass of water.

Father Fonda rapped once and walked into Monsignor's room, surprising him with a button in his mouth. The only light came from the reading lamp over the bed, so that the tall, angular furniture stood in shadows along the walls, giving the room the look of a taxidermist's shop: a large wardrobe stood on its hind legs and a bureau moved stealthily along the wall, stalking a hassock. Father Fonda waved the announcement book in the air and dropped it on the foot of the bed. He walked across the room and fell heavily into the red leather chair and crossed his legs. The elastic of his white sweat socks was broken so that they sat in rings above his shoes like bracelets. Above the socks, his thick hairy legs gave no indication of tapering to ankles.

"You sure you want to take that sermon, Monsignor?"

"Of course I'm sure."

"I mean, I'm prepared and everything."

"You might knock on my door when you go down for the six," Monsignor said. "I don't trust this clock." He picked the clock up and turned it in his hand to see if anything had happened to make it trustworthy. As he set it down he sneaked a look at his palm, careful to keep the other hand closed, the finger tips touching the heel, making a nest.

"Okay, you're the boss," Father Fonda said. As he stood there was a sound like scotch tape being taken up. "You oughta cover this chair with something," he said, turning to look at it.

"I know. These hot nights it gets sticky."

"Not only that. It runs." He held out a beefy hand, palm up. "Look!"

Monsignor propped himself up on his elbows. "What's that?"

"I don't know. Dye, I guess. I hope I didn't get any on me." He grabbed a handful of his skirt and twisted around like a dog chasing its tail. "I guess not." He headed for the door.

"Good night, Monsignor."

"Ah, wait a minute, Father."

Father Fonda stopped with his hand on the door and looked back to the bed where Monsignor had dropped back onto the pillows.

"Yes, Monsignor."

"You said you already prepared a sermon?"

"Sure. On matrimony."

Monsignor fingered his chin thoughtfully.

"Well, maybe you'd better take it then. As long as you're prepared."

"Whatever you say, Monsignor. You're the boss."

After Father Fonda had gone, Monsignor lay staring at the ceiling for several minutes. Finally he reached up and snapped off the light. Through the floor, he heard familiar music, then Marshal Dillon getting off a shot a split second late. Ten o'clock. He had been out of the confessional exactly one hour. He knew he would not go in again in his lifetime.

He shifted himself in the bed so that he would have the pleasure of settling into it again. He closed his eyes, then opened them. In the darkness he looked up at the ceiling.

"You're the boss," he said quietly. Then, quickly and without trying, in the way of children and old people, he went to sleep.

THE BISHOP'S BEGGAR
by Steven Vincent Benet

IT seems that in the old days there was a bishop of Remo, and he was a heedless and proud young man, though of good intentions. Now, that was possible in those days, when the fire and light of the new learning had spread through Italy and men drank, as if intoxicated, at a new spring. There were bishops who cared less for the Word of God than for their own splendor, and cardinals who were rather men of the world—and of no good world—than sons of the Church. I do not say that our bishop was as idle and self-seeking as some of these; I do say that he was a child of his time. He would have liked to be a lord, but his eldest brother was the lord; he would have liked to be a soldier, but his second brother was the soldier. So he went into the Church, for there, too, a man who bore a great name could rise. He was clever, he was ambitious, he had great connections. Now and then, to be sure, he asked a disquieting question, but the Baldis had always been original. The path that is rugged for many was made smooth for him from the first. When he was made bishop of Remo, at an early age, the fact did not surprise him. Since he was to be neither lord nor soldier, he found that pleasant enough.

All went well for him, at first. They were glad to have a young and handsome bishop at Remo, for the bishop before him had been old and ill-favored. It was a pleasure to no one to kiss his ring, and he frightened the children with his peering eyes. With the coming of our bishop all this was changed. There was a great to-do and refurbishing of the bishop's palace; the smells of good cooking drifted again from the bishop's kitchens; when the bishop drove through the city, men threw their caps in the air. There were fine new frescoes in the cathedral—a new way of chanting in the choir. As for sin and suffering—well, they are always with us. The people of Remo liked to sin pleasantly and be reminded of it as little as possible.

Nevertheless, at times, a grayness would come over our bishop's spirit. He could not understand why it came. His life was both full and busy. He was a friend to art, a host to the gay and the learned, a ruler of men. He did not meddle in things which did not concern him; he felt in his heart that there was no prize in the Church which might not be within his grasp. And yet, at times, there was a grayness within him. It was singular.

He could not show that grayness before the world, he could not show it to his secretary or the witty company that gathered at his table. He could wrestle with it in prayer, and so he did. But he found it no easy task. Had the Devil appeared before him with horns and a tail, he would have known what to do. But a grayness of spirit—a cool little voice in the mind which said to him now and then, "What do you in these robes, at this place, Gianfrancesco Baldi?"—that was another matter.

He came to find by experience that motion in the open air helped him as much as anything. When the grayness oppressed him too severely, he would summon his coach and drive about the countryside. So one day, as he drove through a small country village in the hills beyond Remo, it happened. It was nobody's fault; the bishop's least of all. He saw to it that he had a skillful coachman and good horses as he saw to all such matters. But when a tall, gangling boy darts across the street right under the nose of the horses, the most skillful coachman cannot always save him. There was a cry and a scream and a soft jar. Then, where the coach had passed, the boy lay writhing in the street.

The bishop always showed at his best in emergency. When he got out of the coach the angry shouts of the crowd died away to a respectful murmur. He lifted the boy into the coach with his strong arms and drove back with him to Remo. On the way he talked to him soothingly, though the boy was in too much pain to pay much attention to this graciousness. When they got to Remo he had the boy carried to a servant's room in the palace and doctors summoned for him. Later on he gave instructions about cleaning the coach.

At dinner his secretary recounted the little incident and all men praised the kindliness of the bishop. The bishop passed it off pleasantly, but, at heart, he felt a trifle irritated. He had not felt particularly drawn toward the boy; on the other hand, he could not have left him lying in the road.

By the next day, as such things do, the story had gone all over Remo and there were unusual demonstrations of good will as the bishop passed to the cathedral. The bishop received them with dignity, but his irritation remained. He disliked ostentatious shows of virtue and distrusted the fickleness of crowds. Nevertheless, it was his duty to see the boy, and he did so.

Washed, combed and rid of his vermin, the boy looked ordinary enough, though somewhat older than the bishop had thought him. His body was slight and emaciated, but he had a well-shaped head and large liquid eyes. These stared at the bishop with some intensity; indeed with such intensity that the bishop wondered, at first, if the boy might not be an idiot. But a little conversation proved him sound of mind, though rustic in speech.

His name was Luigi and he was an orphan, living as best he could. In the summer he tended goats; in the winter he lived with his uncle and aunt, the tavern keepers, who fed him and beat him. His age was about nineteen. He had made his Easter duty as a Christian. He would never walk again.

Such were the facts of the case, and the bishop thought them over clear-headedly. He wondered what to do with the boy.

"Luigi," he said, "would you like to go back to your village?"

"Oh, no," said the boy. "It is a very good village, but now that I can no longer herd goats, there is no place in it for me. Besides, one eats better in Remo—I have had white cheese twice already." And he smacked his lips. His voice was remarkably strong and cheerful, the bishop noticed with surprise.

"Very well," said the bishop patiently. "You need not go back if you do not choose. You are now, in some sense, a ward of the Church, and the wings of the Church are sheltering." He looked at the boy's legs, lying limp and motionless under the covers, and felt, though against his will, the natural distaste of the hale man for the maimed. "You might learn some useful trade," he said thoughtfully. "There are many trades where the hands do all—a cobbler's, a tailor's, a basket weaver's."

The boy shook his head joyfully. "Oh, no,

your lordship," he said. "Trades take so long to learn and I am very stupid. It would not be worth the expense; your lordship would be embarrassed."

"My lordship, perhaps, is the best judge of that," said the bishop a trifle grimly. He kept thinking of the boy's remark about white cheese; it must be a spare life indeed where white cheese was such a treat. "But we are reasonable," he said. "Come, what would you be?"

"A beggar!" said the boy, and his dark eyes shone with delight.

"A beggar?" said the bishop, astonished and somewhat revolted.

"Why, yes," said the boy, as if it were the most natural thing in the world. "For ten years my father begged on the cathedral steps. That was before your lordship's time, but he was an excellent beggar and a master of his craft. True, he was subject to continual persecution and jealousies from the honorable corporation of the beggars of Remo, coming, as he did, from outside the city. It was that which caused the ruin of our fortunes, for, in the end, when he had begun to fail, they threw him down a well, where he caught a bad cold and died of it. But in his good days he could outbeg any two of them. If your lordship would care to have me demonstrate his celebrated fainting fit, when his eyeballs rolled backward in his head——"

"I can think of nothing I should like less," said the bishop, shocked and disgusted, for it seemed to him an unworthy thing that a sturdy young man, though a cripple, should think of nothing better than beggary. "Besides," he said, "these other beggars you speak of—if they persecuted your father, no doubt they would persecute you."

"Me?" said the boy, and laughed. "Oh, once they understood, they would not dare touch me—not even Giuseppe, the Hook. I would be your lordship's beggar—the bishop's beggar!" And a light as of great peace and contentment spread over his countenance.

The bishop stared at him for a long time in silence. "That is what you wish?" he said, and his voice was dry.

"That is what I wish, your lordship," said the boy, nodding his head.

"So be it," said the bishop with a sigh, and left him. But when his coachman came to him the next morning for orders, it was all he could do to keep from reviling the man.

The bishop was not the sort of man who liked beggars. Indeed, were it not for custom and Christian charity, he would long since have cleared them from the steps of his cathedral. He could not very well do that; he knew what an impression such a move would make. Nevertheless, when he passed among them, as he must at times, he saw to it that his almoner made a suitable distribution of small coins, but he himself did his best to see and smell them as little as possible. Their whines and their supplications, their simulated sores and their noisome rags—these were a fret and a burden to him.

Now it seemed, he was to have a beggar of his own. He would have taken it as a suitable humiliation for pride, but he did not feel himself to be a proud man. Nor could he think of the accident as anything but an accident. Had he deliberately trodden the lad beneath the hoofs of his horses—but he had not. He was well liked, able, decisive, a rising son of the Church. Nevertheless, he was to have a beggar—every day he must see his beggar on the steps of the cathedral, a living reproach, a living lesson in idleness and heedlessness. It was a small thing, to be sure, but it darkened his dinner and made him sore at heart.

Therefore, being the man he was, he put a mask upon his face. He meant to speak of the thing, so it should be known—at least that might ward off ridicule. He spoke of it to his secretary; the secretary agreed that it was a very seemly and Christian idea of his lordship's, while the bishop wondered if the man laughed at him in his sleeve. He spoke of it to others; there were compliments, of course. Each time he spoke of it, it turned a small knife in his breast. But that did not keep him from speaking of it, nor from seeing that every care was given Luigi.

Nevertheless, he dreaded the day when Luigi would take up his post on the steps of the cathedral. He dreaded and yearned for it, both. For then, at last, the thing would be done. After that, like many things, it would become a custom, and in time Luigi himself would fade into the mass of whining beggary that haunted the steps of the cathedral. But things were not to be quite that way.

He admired, while he detested, the thoroughness with which Luigi prepared himself for his profession. He heard the whine ring out from the servants' quarters—"ten scudi for Luigi!"—he saw the little cart and the crutches Luigi had made for himself. Now and then he heard his own servants laugh at the beggar's stories. This was hard enough to bear. But at last the day of parting came.

To his disgust, the bishop found the boy neither clean nor well clad, as he had been since his accident, but dirty and dressed in tatters. He opened his mouth to reprove the boy, then he shut it again, for it seemed pitifully true that a beggar must dress his part. Nevertheless, the bishop did not like it. He asked Luigi, cooly, how he meant to live.

"Oh, your lordship's secretary has found me a very suitable chamber," said Luigi eagerly. "It is on the ground floor of a rookery by the river and it has room for my crutches, my gear and my cart. He will move me there tonight. Tomorrow I will be at my post on the steps of the cathedral." And he smiled gratefully at the bishop. "That will be a great day," he said.

"So," said the bishop, who could not trust himself to say anything further.

"Yet before I go," said Luigi, "I must thank your lordship for his kindness, and ask your lordship's blessing on my work. That is only suitable."

The bishop stiffened. "I may bless you, Luigi," he said, "but your work I cannot bless. I cannot give the blessing of the Church to the work of a man who lives by beggary when he might live otherwise."

"Well, then, I must go unblessed," said Luigi cheerfully. "After all, your lordship has already done so much for me! The bishop's beggar! How my uncle and aunt will stare!"

Now, of all the vainglorious, self-seeking, worthless, rascally sons of iniquity—and to think that I stand your sponsor, said the bishop, but, fortunately, he did not say it aloud. Silently he extended his ring and Luigi kissed it with such innocent reverence that the bishop was sorely moved to give him his blessing after all. But he summoned up his principles and departed in silence.

The bishop slept ill that night, tormented by dreams of Luigi. He dreamed that, for his sins, he must carry Luigi on his back all the way up the steps of the cathedral. And as he mounted each step the weight upon his back became more crushing, till at last he woke, unrefreshed.

The next day he went to the cathedral in great state, though it was an ordinary Sunday. Yet he felt the state to be, in some measure, a protection. When he passed by the steps of the cathedral, the beggars set up their usual supplications. He sent his almoner among them; it was over quicker than he thought. He did not look for Luigi and yet he felt Luigi's eyes upon him as he stood there for a moment, splendid in robe and miter. Then the thing was finished.

In the cathedral that same day, he preached passionately against the sins of idleness and heedlessness. Seldom had he been so moving—he could feel that from his congregation. When Mass was over he retired to his palace, exhausted. Yet it was pleasant for him to walk about the palace and know that Luigi was not there.

It was just after vespers when his secretary came to him and told him that a man called Giuseppe, self-styled provost of the company of the beggars of Remo, requested an audience. The bishop sighed wearily and ordered the man brought before him. He was a squat fellow of great strength and an evil cast of countenance, for one side of his face had been so burned in a fire that it was as if he had two faces, one of them inhuman. Also, his left arm terminated in an iron hook.

"This is Giuseppe, the beggar, your lordship," said the secretary, with repugnance.

"Giuseppe, called Double-Face, also called the Hook, provost of the honorable company of the beggars of Remo," said Giuseppe in a rusty voice, and plumped on his knees.

The bishop raised him and asked his business.

"Well, your lordship, it's this new fellow, Luigi Lamelegs," said Giuseppe. "I've got nothing against him personal—I wouldn't hurt a fly myself in a personal way," and he grinned horribly—"but there he is in a good place on the steps, and your lordship's servants put him there. Well, now, if he's your lordship's beggar, that's one thing—though, even so, there's fees and vails to be paid, for that's the custom. But if he isn't your lordship's beggar—and your lordship paid him no attention this morning—"

"Stop!" said the bishop with anger. "Do you mean to tell me that the very steps of the cathedral are bartered and sold among you? Why, this is simony—this is the sin of simony!"

"Your lordship can call it hard words," said Giuseppe stolidly, "but that's been the way it's been done ever since there were beggars in Remo.

I paid twenty crowns for my own place, and fought old Marco too. But that's beside the point. Your lordship has a right to a beggar if your lordship wants one—we're all agreed on that. But the question is: Is this man your lordship's beggar or isn't he?"

"And supposing I said he was not my beggar?" said the bishop, trembling.

"Well, that's all we'd want to know," said Giuseppe. "And thank your lordship kindly. I had my own suspicions of the man from the first. But we've got him down by the river now—Carlo and Benito and old blind Marta; she's a tough one, old blind Marta—and once we're through with him, he'll trouble your lordship no more." And sketching a clumsy salute, the man turned to go.

"Stop!" said the bishop again. "Would you have the guilt of murder upon your conscience?"

"Oh, your lordship takes it too hard," said Giuseppe, shuffling his feet. "What's one beggar more or less? We're not rich folk or learned folk to bother a mind like your lordship's. We breed and we die, and there's an end. And even at the best, it's no bed of roses on the steps of the cathedral."

The bishop wished to say many things, but he could think of only one.

"I declare to you that this man is my beggar," he said. "I stretch my hand over him."

"Well, that's very nicely spoken of your lordship," said Giuseppe, in a grumbling voice, "and I dare say we can make room for him. But if the man's to keep a whole skin, your lordship had best come with me—old Marta was talking of ear-slitting when I left her."

So they found Luigi, bound but cheerful, in his first-floor chamber by the river, guarded by the persons Giuseppe had described—a hunchback, a dwarf and a blind woman. The window which gave upon the river was open, and a large sack, weighted with stones, lay in one corner of the room. The bishop's arrival produced a certain consternation on the part of all but Luigi, who seemed to take it as a matter of course. After the boy had been unbound the bishop addressed the beggars with some vivacity, declared that Luigi was his beggar, and gave him a piece of silver before them all, in token. This seemed to satisfy the company, who then crept away in silence.

"And yet have I done right? Have I done right?" said the bishop, striding up and down the chamber. "I greatly fear I have condoned the sin of simony! I have spent Mother Church's substance among the unworthy! And yet, even so, your blood may be upon my head!" and he looked at Luigi doubtfully.

"Oh, your lordship need not take it so hard," said Luigi, rubbing his arms. "All is safe enough now. I arranged about the dues and vails with Giuseppe while your lordship was discussing her state of grace with Marta. He's an honest fellow enough and his point is reasonable. One should not take a good place without money to keep it up. Had your lordship given me alms with your own hand this morning, our little difficulty would never have arisen. That was my fault—I assumed that your lordship knew."

"Knew?" said the bishop. "What should I know of such things? And yet, God forgive me, I am a priest and I should have knowledge of evil."

"It is merely a difference in knowledge," said Luigi gently. "Now, your lordship, doubtless, has never been in a room quite like this before."

The bishop stared at the damp walls and the mean chamber. He smelled the smell that cannot be aired from a room, the smell of poverty itself. He had never doubted his own experience before—when he had been first made a priest, he had gone on certain works of charity. Now it seemed to him that those works must have been rather carefully selected.

"No," he said, "I have never been in a room just like this one."

"And yet there are many of us who live in such rooms—and not all beggars," said Luigi. He changed his tone. "That was a fine rousing sermon your lordship gave us on idleness and heedlessness this morning," he said. "Hey, it brought the scudi forth from the good folks' pockets! An admirable sermon!"

"I am grateful for your encomiums," said the bishop bitterly. He glanced around the room again. "Is there nought else I can do?" he said unwillingly.

"No, thank your lordship," said Luigi, and his eyes were smiling. "I have a woman to cook my dinner—it is true she is a thief, but she will not steal from a cripple—and soon, with your lordship's patronage, I shall be able to afford a charcoal brazier. Moreover, my friends seem to have left me a sack. So, after dinner I shall say my prayers and go to bed to refresh myself for tomorrow's labor."

I shall say mine, too, for I need them, said the bishop, though he did not say it to Luigi.

So that was how it began. Soon enough, the bishop's beggar was a familiar figure on the steps of the cathedral—one of the admitted curiosities of the town. He was well liked in his trade, for he always had a merry word or a sharp one for his clients—and it passed around until "Luigi says" became a byword. The bishop became used to him as one becomes used to a touch of rheumatism. Other men had their difficulties; he had his beggar. Now and then it seemed odd to the bishop that he had ever thought of the beggars on the steps as a vague and indistinguishable heap of misery and rags. He knew them all by now—blind Marta and Carlo, the dwarf, Giuseppe Double-Face, and Benito, the hunchback. He knew their ways and their thoughts. He knew the hovels where they lived and the bread they ate. For every week or so he would slip from his palace to visit Luigi's chamber.

It was necessary for him to do so, for, to him, Luigi represented the gravest problem of the soul that he had yet encountered. Was the man even a Christian? The bishop was not sure. He professed religion, he followed the rites of the Church. Yet sometimes when he confessed him, the bishop was appalled. Every sin that could ravage the human heart was there—if not in act, then in desire—and all told so gaily! Sometimes the bishop, angrily, would tax him with willful exaggeration, and Luigi, with a smile, would admit the charge and ask for still another penance. This left the bishop confused.

Yet through the years there grew up between the two men a singular bond. The bishop may have been heedless, he was not stupid. Very soon he began to realize that there was another Remo than the city he had come to first—a city not of lords and scholars and tradesmen and pious ladies, but a city of the poor and the ignorant, the maimed and the oppressed. For as Luigi said, when one lay all day on the steps of the cathedral one heard stories, and anyone will talk to a beggar. Some of the stories struck the bishop to the heart. He could hardly believe them at first, yet, when he investigated them, they were true. When he was convinced they were true, he set himself stubbornly to remedy them. He was not always successful—pleasant sinners like the Church to keep its own place. Now and then he discussed his efforts with Luigi, who listened, it seemed to the bishop, with an air of perfect cynicism. His attitude seemed to be that it was all very well for a man like the bishop to concern himself about these things, but he was the bishop's beggar and, if other folk starved and died, it was none of his concern. This irritated the bishop inordinately and made him more determined than ever.

Gradually, he noticed, the composition of his table changed. There were fewer courtiers and scholars; there were more priests from the country, smelling of poverty and chestnut bread. They came in their tattered cassocks, with their big red wrists; at first they were strange and ill-at-ease at his table. But the bishop was able to talk to them. After all, were they not like the old parish priest that Luigi talked of so often? When the ceremony of his table disturbed them he saw to it that there was less ceremony. Luigi mocked him for this and told him bluntly what his richer clients were saying. The bishop rebuked him for impertinence to his spiritual director and persisted.

It is strange how time flies when the heart is occupied. In no time at all, it seemed to the bishop, he was a middle-aged man with gray at his temples, and Luigi a man in his thirties. That seemed odd to the bishop; he did not know where the time had gone. He thought of it, one morning, with a sense of loss. He had meant to do many things—he was still ambitious. Now, when night came, he was often too tired to think. The troubles of many people weighed upon his heart—the troubles of the peasants in the hills, who lived from hand to mouth; the trouble of Domenico, the shoemaker, who had too pretty a daughter; the troubles of Tessa, the flower seller, whose son was a thief. When he had first come to Remo, he had not had all these troubles. He picked up a letter on his desk—a letter that had lain there for days—and, having read it, sat staring.

The dreams of his youth came back to him, doubly hot, doubly dear. While he idled his life away in Remo his brother and his friends had been busy. They had not forgotten him, after all. Cardinal Malaverni, the great sage statesman whose hand was ever upon the strings of policy, meant to pass by Remo on his way to Rome. The bishop knew the cardinal—once, long ago, he had been one of the cardinal's promising young men. There was a letter also from the bishop's brother, the lord—a letter that hinted of grave and important matters. The bishop almost sobbed when he thought how long both letters had lain unanswered. He summoned his secretary and set himself about an unaccustomed bustle of preparation.

It often occurred to him, sorrowfully, within the next few days, how foolish it was to leave one's letters unopened. The preparations went forward for the cardinal's visit, yet it seemed to him that they went forward ill, though he could not put his finger upon the cause. Somehow he had got out of the way of the world where such things go forward smoothly; he was more used to his country priests than to entertaining distinguished visitors. Nevertheless, he botched together a few Latin verses, saw to it that the hangings in the guest chambers were cleaned and mended, drove his choirmaster nearly frantic and got in the way of his servants. He noticed that these were no longer afraid of him, but treated him with tolerant patience, more like a friend than a master, and this irked him oddly. What irked him even more, perhaps, was Luigi's shameless and undisguised self-interest in the whole affair.

"Ah, your lordship, we've waited a long time for this," he said, "but it's come at last. And everyone knows that a great man like Cardinal Malaverni doesn't come to a place like Remo for nothing. So all we have to do is play our cards well, and then, when we move on, as we doubtless shall—well, I, for one, won't be sorry."

"Move on?" said the bishop, astonished.

The beggar yawned.

"But how else?" he said. "I have been the bishop's beggar. When your lordship is made a cardinal I will be the cardinal's beggar. The post will entail new responsibilities, no doubt, but I have confidence in my abilities. Perhaps I shall even employ an assistant for my actual begging—after all, it is often drafty on the steps of the cathedral."

The bishop turned and left him without a word. Yet what Luigi had said caused trouble and disquiet in his heart, for he knew that Luigi often had news of things to come before even the Count of Remo had an inkling of them.

At last the great day of the cardinal's visit came.

Like all such days, it passed as a dream passes, with heat and ceremony and worry about small things. The Latin verses of welcome were unexpectedly well read; on the other hand, the choristers were nervous and did not sing their best. Two gentlemen of the cardinal's suite had to be lodged over the stables, much to the bishop's distress, and the crayfish for dinner had been served without sauce.

The bishop hoped that all had gone well, but he did not know. As he sat, at last, alone with his old friend in his study that overlooked the garden, he felt at once wrought-up and drowsy.

This should be the real pleasure of the day, to sit with his old friend in the cool of the evening and renew contact with the great world. But the bishop was used to country hours by now and the feast had broken up late. He should be listening to the cardinal with the greatest attention, and yet those accursed crayfish kept coming into his mind.

"Well, Gianfrancesco," said the cardinal, sipping delicately at his wine, "you have given your old tutor a most charming welcome. Your wine, your people, your guests—it reminds me somehow of one of those fine Virgilian eclogues we used to parse together. *'Tityre, tu patulae recubans—'*"

"The choir," said the bishop, "the choir usually is—"

"Why, they sang very well!" said the cardinal. "And what good, honest, plain-spoken priests you have in your charge!" He shook his head sadly. "I fear that we do not always get their like in Rome. And yet, each man to his task."

"They have a hard charge in these hills," said the bishop wearily. "It was a great honor for them to see Your Eminence."

"Oh, honor!" said the cardinal. "To see an old man with the gout—yes, I have the gout these days, Gianfrancesco—I fear we both are not so young as we were." He leaned forward and regarded the bishop attentively. "You, too, have altered, my old friend," he said softly.

"Your Eminence means that I have rusticated," said the bishop a trifle bitterly. "Well, it is true."

"Oh, not rusticated," said the cardinal, with a charming gesture. "Not at all. But there has been a change—a perceptible one—from the Gianfrancesco I knew." He took a walnut and began to crack it. "That Gianfrancesco was a charming and able young man," he said. "Yet I doubt if he would have made the count of his city do penance in his shirt, for his sins, before the doors of the cathedral."

"I can explain about that," said the bishop hurriedly. "The shirt was a silk one and the weather by no means inclement. Moreover, the count's new tax would have ruined my poor. It is true we have not always seen eye to eye since then, yet I think he respects me more than he did before."

"That is just what I said to your brother, Piero," said the cardinal comfortably. "I said, 'You are wrong to be perturbed about this, Piero; it will have a good effect.' Yes, even as regards the beggar."

"My beggar?" said the bishop, and sighed.

"Oh, you know how small things get about," said the cardinal. "Some small thing is seized upon; it even travels to Rome. The bishop's beggar—the beggar's bishop—the bishop who humbles his soul to protect the poor."

"But it was not like that at all," said the bishop. "I—"

The cardinal waved him aside. "Do not hide your good works beneath a bushel, Gianfrancesco," he said. "The Church herself has need of them. These are troubled times we live in. The French king may march any day. There is heresy and dissension abroad. You have no idea what difficult days may lie ahead." He watched the bishop intently. "Our Holy Father leans much upon my unworthy shoulder," he said, "and our Holy Father is beginning to age."

"That is sore news for us all," said the bishop.

"Sore indeed," said the cardinal. "And yet, one must face realities. Should our Holy Father die, it will be necessary for those of us who truly love the Church to stand together—more especially in the college of cardinals." He paused and with a silver nutpick extracted the last meat from the walnut. "I believe that our Holy Father is disposed to reward your own labors with the see of Albano," he said.

"The see of Albano?" said the bishop as if in a dream, for, as all men knew, Albano was an old and famous diocese outside the walls of Rome and he who was bishop of Albano wore a cardinal's hat.

"It might have a most excellent effect," said the cardinal. "I myself think it might. We have clever and able men who are sons of the Church. Indeed. And yet, just at this moment, with both the French and the German parties so active—well, there is perhaps need for another sort of man—at least as regards the people." He smiled delightfully. "You would be very close to me as cardinal-bishop of Albano—very close to us all," he said. "I should lean upon you, Gianfrancesco."

"There is nought that would please me more!" cried the bishop, like a boy. He thought for a moment of the power and the glory, of the great, crowded streets of Rome and the Church that humbles kings. "I would have to leave Remo?" he said.

"Well, yes, naturally, it would mean your having to leave Remo," said the cardinal. "Your new duties would demand it."

"That would be hard," said the bishop. "I would have to leave Luigi and all my people." He thought of them suddenly—the lame, the halt, the oppressed.

"Your people, perhaps," said the cardinal, "but certainly not Luigi. He should come with you by all means, as a living example."

"Oh, no, no, that would never do," said the bishop. "Your Eminence does not understand. Luigi is difficult enough, as a bishop's beggar.

As a cardinal's beggar, he would be overweening. You have no idea how overweening he would be."

The cardinal regarded him with a puzzled stare.

"Am I dreaming, Gianfrancesco?" he said. "Or are you declining the see of Albano and a cardinal's hat for no more reason than that you are attached to a beggar?"

"Oh, no, no, no!" cried the bishop, in an agony. "I am not in the least attached to him—he is my cross and my thorn. But you see, it would be so bad for him if I were to be made a cardinal. I tremble to think what would happen to his soul. And then there are all his companions—Giuseppe, the Hook, is dead, but there is still blind Marta, and Benito, the hunchback, and the new ones. No, I must stay in Remo."

The cardinal smiled—a smile of exasperation. "I think you have forgotten something, Gianfrancesco," he said. "I think you have forgotten that obedience is the first law of the Church."

"I am five times obedient," said the bishop. "Let our Holy Father do with me as he wills. Let him send me as a missionary to savages; let him strip me of my bishopric and set me to work in the hills. I shall be content. But while I have been given Remo, I have work to do in Remo. I did not expect it to be so when I first came here," he said in a low voice, "and yet, somehow, I find that it is so."

The cardinal said nothing at all for a long time.

Then at last he rose, and, pressing the bishop's hand, he retired to his own quarters. The bishop hoped that he was comfortable in them, though it occurred to him, in the uneasy sleep before dawn, that the chimney smoked.

Next morning the cardinal departed on his journey toward Rome without speaking of these matters further. The bishop felt sorry to see him go, and yet relieved. He had been very glad to see his old friend again—he told himself that. Yet from the moment of the cardinal's arrival there had been an unfamiliar grayness upon his spirit, and now that grayness was gone. Nevertheless, he knew that he must face Luigi—and that thought was hard for him.

Yet it went well enough, on the whole.

The bishop explained to him, as one explains to a child, that it did not seem as if God had intended him to be a cardinal, only bishop of Remo, and with that Luigi had to be content. He grumbled about it frequently and remarked that if he had known all this in the first place, he might never have accepted the position of bishop's beggar. But he was not any more overweening than before, and with that the bishop had to be satisfied.

Then came the war with the French, and that was hard upon the bishop. He did not like wars, he did not like the thought of his people being killed. Yet, when the Count of Remo fled with most of his soldiery, and the mayor locked himself in his house and stayed there, shaking, there was no one to take over the rule of the town but the bishop. The very beggars in the streets cried out for him; he could not escape the task.

He took it with a heavy heart, under the mocking eyes of Luigi. With Luigi in his cart, he inspected the walls and defenses.

"Well, your lordship has a very great problem," said Luigi. "Half a dozen good cannon shot and the city will be taken by storm."

"I thought so, I feared so," said the bishop, sighing. "And yet my people are my people."

"Your lordship might easily compromise with the enemy," said Luigi. "They are angry with the count, it is true—they thought they had him bought over. Yet it would mean but two score hangings or so, and a tribute, properly assessed."

"I cannot permit my flock to be harried and persecuted," said the bishop.

"Well, if your lordship must die, I will die with your lordship," said Luigi. "Meanwhile, we might set the townsfolk to work on the walls—at least it will give them something to do. And yet, there may be another way."

So it was done and the bishop worked day and night, enheartening and encouraging his people. For once, all Remo was one, and the spirit and will that burned within it were the bishop's. Yet it seemed no time at all before the French sat down before Remo.

They sent a trumpet and a flag to demand the surrender of the city. The bishop received the young officer who came with the trumpet—a dark-faced man he was, with a humorous twist to his mouth. The bishop even took him on a tour of the walls, which seemed to surprise him a little.

"You are well defended," said the Frenchman politely.

"Oh, no, we are very ill defended," said the bishop. "My good children have been trying to strengthen the wall with sandbags, but, as you perceive, it is rotten and needs rebuilding. Moreover, the count was badly cheated on his powder. I must speak to him of it sometime, for hardly a gun we have is fit to fire."

The Frenchman's astonishment grew. "I do not wish to doubt your lordship's word," he said, "but if those things are so, how does your lordship propose to defend Remo?"

"By the will of God," said the bishop very simply. "I do not wish my poor people killed; neither do I wish them oppressed. If needs must, I shall die in their stead, but they shall go scatheless. Ere you hang one man of Remo, I shall take the noose from around his neck and put it around my own."

"Your lordship makes things very difficult," said the Frenchman thoughtfully. "My king has no desire to attack the Church—and, indeed, the walls of Remo seem stronger than your lordship reckons."

Then he was conscious of a plucking at his sleeve. It was Luigi, the beggar, in his little cart, who, by signs and grimaces, seemed to wish the Frenchman to follow him.

"What is it, Luigi?" said the bishop wearily. "Ah, yes, you wish to show our friend the room where we store the powder. Very well. Then he may see how little we have."

When the Frenchman rejoined the bishop, he was wiping sweat from his forehead and his face was white. The bishop pressed him to stay for a glass of wine, but he said he must return to his camp, and departed, muttering something incoherent about it being indeed the will of God that defended Remo.

When he had gone, the bishop looked severely upon Luigi. "Luigi," he said sternly, "I fear you have been up to some of your tricks."

"How your lordship mistakes me," said the beggar. "It is true I showed him three of my fellow-beggars—and they did not seem to him in the best of health. But I did not say they had plague; I let him draw his own conclusions. It took me four days to school them in their parts, but that I did not tell him either."

"That was hardly honest, Luigi," said the bishop. "We know there is no plague in the town."

"We know also that our walls are rotten," said Luigi, "but the French will not believe that, either. Men of war are extremely suspicious—it is their weakness. We shall wait and see."

They waited and saw, for that night a council of war was held in the French camp and the officer who had come with the trumpet reported (a) that Remo was held in great force and strongly defended; (b) that its bishop was resolved to die in the breach, and (c) that there was plague in the city. Taking all these factors into account, the French wisely decided, after some forty-eight hours' delay, to strike camp and fall back on their main army—which they did just in time to take part in the historic defeat of the whole French invasion a week later. This defeat sealed for all time the heroic defense of Remo; for, had the part of the French army occupied before Remo rejoined their main body before, the historic defeat might have been as historic a victory for the French. As it was, all Italy rang with the name of the bishop of Remo.

But of all this the bishop knew nothing, for his beggar, Luigi, was dying.

As the French moved away they had loosed off a few cannon shot, more in irritation than for any real military purpose. However, one of the cannon shot, heedlessly aimed, struck the steps of the cathedral, and you may still see the scars. It also struck the cart wherein Luigi lay, directing his beggars at one task of defense or another. When the bishop first heard that his beggar was hurt, he went to him at once. But there was little that man could do but wait, and the waiting was long. It was not until seven weeks later that Luigi passed from this earth. He endured, indeed, till the messengers came from Rome.

After they had talked with the bishop, the bishop went alone to his cathedral and prayed. Then he went to see Luigi.

"Well?" said the dying man eagerly, staring at him with limpid eyes.

"His Holiness has been graciously pleased to make of me the first archbishop of Remo, placing under my staff, as well, the dioceses of Ugri and Soneto," said the bishop slowly. "But I have the news from Cardinal Malaverni, and I may remain here till I die." He stared at Luigi. "I do not understand," he said.

"It is well done. You have stood by the poor in their poverty and the wretched in their hour of trial," said Luigi, and for once there was no trace of mockery in his voice.

"I do not understand. I do not understand at all," said the bishop again. "And yet I think you deserve recompense rather than I, Luigi."

"No," said Luigi, "that I do not."

The bishop passed his hand across his brow. "I am not a fool," he said. "It was well done, to humble my spirit. And yet, why did you do so, Luigi?"

"Why, that was my great sin," said Luigi. "I have confessed many vain and imaginary sins, but never the real one till now." He paused, as if the words hurt him. "When your lordship's coach rolled over my legs, I was very bitter," he said. "A poor man has little. To lose that little—to lose the air on the hills and the springing step, to lie like a log forever because a bishop's coachman was careless—that made me very bitter. I had rather your lordship had driven over me again than taken me back to your palace and treated me with kindness. I hated your lordship for your indifferent kindness—I hated you for everything."

"Did you so, Luigi?" said the bishop.

"Yes," said Luigi. "And I could see that your lordship hated me—or, if not hated, loathed, like a crippled dog that one must be kind to without liking. So I set myself out to tease and torment your lordship—at first by being your beggar, then in other ways. I could not believe in goodness; I could not believe there would not come a moment when your lordship would turn upon me and drive me forth."

He paused a moment and wiped his mouth with a cloth.

"Yes, I could not believe that at all," he said. "But you were not to be broken, Gianfrancesco, my brother. The evil I showed you daily was like a knife in your heart and a burden on your back, but you bore the knife and the burden. I took delight in showing you how ill things went in your city—how, below the fair surface, there was misery and pain. And had you once turned aside from that misery and pain, I would have been satisfied, for then, bishop or no bishop, you would have lost your soul. Was that evil of me, Gianfrancesco?"

"Very evil in intent," said the bishop steadily, "for, while it is permitted to be tempted, it is evil to tempt. And yet proceed."

"Well," said Luigi, with a sudden childlike stare, "it did not work. The more I tried to make you a bad man, the better man you became. You would not do what was ill; you would not depart from your poor, once you had known them—not even for a red hat or a count's favor. You would not do ill at all. So now we have defended Remo, the two of us, and I am dying." He stirred uneasily in his bed. "It is just as well," he said, with a trace of his old mockery. "I told my uncle I would live to be a cardinal's beggar, but I am not sure that I would have liked it. I have loved you also, Gianfrancesco. Will you give me your blessing now, on me and my work—the blessing you denied me once?"

The bishop's face was wrung. Yet he lifted his hand and absolved and blessed Luigi. He blessed Luigi and his work in the name of the Father and of the Son and of the Holy Ghost. When that had been done, a smile appeared on Luigi's face.

"A very fine blessing," he said. "I must tell that to the Hook when I see him; he will be envious. I wonder is it drafty on the steps of heaven? A very fine blessing, your lordship...ten...scudi...for...Luigi." And with that his jaw dropped and it was over. But the bishop knelt beside the bed with streaming eyes.

And all that, to be sure, was a long time ago. But they still tell the story in Remo when they show the bishop's tomb. He lies upon it, fairly carven in marble. But carved all around the tomb are a multitude of beggars, lame, halt and misshapen, yet all praising God. And there are words in Latin which say, "It is not enough to have knowledge—these also are my sheep." Of the tomb of Luigi, the beggar—that no man knows. They say it was beside the bishop's but, in one war or another, it was destroyed and there is no trace of it now. Yet Luigi was an arrogant spirit; perhaps he would have liked that best.